THE FORTUNES OF TEXAS

*Follow the lives and loves of a complex family
with a rich history and deep ties
in the Lone Star State*

SECRETS OF FORTUNE'S GOLD RANCH

Welcome to Fortune's Gold Ranch...where the vistas of Emerald Ridge are as expansive as the romantic entanglements that beckon its visitors!

FAKING IT WITH A FORTUNE

Poppy Fortune's world turns topsy-turvy the moment a baby appears unexpectedly on her parents' doorstep. Especially when avowed bachelor Leo Leonetti dives in to become her partner in parenting. Leo wants to prove to his grandfather that he cares for more than the family business. What he didn't bargain on? Becoming besotted—again—with a woman who was always more than just a fling...

Dear Reader,

I'm so excited to be part of the Fortunes of Texas family once again this year. We have such a talented group of authors bringing you fun, emotional, heartwarming stories with a deliciously complicated new family and setting in the series.

Welcome to Emerald Ridge, Texas, and the Fortune's Gold Ranch! My story starts off with a bang—or more specifically with a sweet baby left on the front porch of the Fortune family. Newly certified foster parent Poppy Fortune might not be lucky in love, but she's committed to loving the boy named Joey until they discover the mystery of his parents' identity.

Turns out being a single mom is more of a challenge than Poppy expects, and when her former boyfriend Leo Leonetti steps up to help, she finds herself forging a partnership she never expected.

Leo admires Poppy's dedication but gets involved with baby Joey to make his beloved grandfather happy. However, Leo and Poppy quickly discover that playing at being a family feels far too real when their hearts get involved.

I hope you love this journey to happily-ever-after as much as I loved writing it!

Big hugs,

Michelle

FAKING IT WITH A FORTUNE

MICHELLE MAJOR

Harlequin

THE FORTUNES OF TEXAS

Special thanks and acknowledgment are given to
Michelle Major for her contribution to
The Fortunes of Texas: Secrets of Fortune's Gold Ranch miniseries.

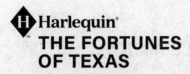 **Harlequin®**
THE FORTUNES
OF TEXAS

Recycling programs
for this product may
not exist in your area.

ISBN-13: 978-1-335-99678-7

Faking It with a Fortune

Copyright © 2025 by Harlequin Enterprises ULC

 Harlequin Enterprises ULC
22 Adelaide St. West, 41st Floor
Toronto, Ontario M5H 4E3, Canada
www.Harlequin.com

Printed in Lithuania

MIX
Paper | Supporting
responsible forestry
www.fsc.org   FSC® C021394

Michelle Major grew up in Ohio but dreamed of living in the mountains. Soon after graduating with a degree in journalism, she pointed her car west and settled in Colorado. Her life and house are filled with one great husband, two beautiful kids, a few furry pets and several well-behaved reptiles. She's grateful to have found her passion writing stories with happy endings. Michelle loves to hear from her readers at michellemajor.com.

Books by Michelle Major

The Fortunes of Texas: Digging for Secrets

Fortune's Baby Claim

The Fortunes of Texas: Secrets of Fortune's Gold Ranch

Faking It with a Fortune

Harlequin Special Edition

Welcome to Starlight

The Best Intentions
The Last Man She Expected
His Secret Starlight Baby
Starlight and the Single Dad

Crimson, Colorado

Anything for His Baby
A Baby and a Betrothal
Always the Best Man
Christmas on Crimson Mountain
Romancing the Wallflower

For additional books by Michelle Major,
visit her website, michellemajor.com

To the authors and readers of the Fortunes of Texas family.
Everything's bigger and better in Texas!

Chapter One

Poppy Fortune blinked back tears as she read the words needlepointed into the square throw pillow she'd just unwrapped. "'Love lives here,'" she whispered as she met her mother's gaze across the kitchen table. "It's perfect. Thank you, Mom."

Shelley Fortune swiped a hand across her cheek. "I'm so proud of you, sweetie. I hope the pillow reminds you who you are and what an amazing thing you've done."

"I haven't done anything yet," Poppy countered with a smile. "The real accomplishment will be when I have a child placed with me. Laura, my caseworker, said it could take anywhere from two days to two months now that I'm official."

It had taken several months for her to become approved as a foster parent. She had to balance the hours needed to complete the training with her demanding job running the spa at Fortune's Gold Ranch, the property her family had owned for decades in the upscale town of Emerald Ridge, Texas. The spa was always busy over the holidays. Clients wanted preparty pampering or to unwind during the busy season. Bookings had remained steady through the first couple weeks of January, but it was Februrary now, and the winter lull was officially upon them.

The social service caseworker had completed Poppy's home visit earlier in the week, and she'd received word today that she'd been approved. Her mom, the only member of her family who seemed to take her desire to be a foster parent seriously, had insisted on a congratulatory dinner.

Poppy's father, Garth, was out of town until the following morning. Her brothers, Rafe and Shane, were busy with their own lives, so it was a girls' night, which she and her mom didn't have nearly enough of anymore.

"We're celebrating your decision and dedication to helping kids who need a safe place to stay." Shelley rose from her chair and went to stir the mushroom risotto, Poppy's favorite, simmering on the stove.

She adored her dad and brothers, but they didn't understand or appreciate her desire to become a foster parent. Maybe the same could be said for her mom, but at least Shelley made her feel supported no matter what path she took.

That was something she wanted to offer the children who came into her life through this endeavor. Growing up in Emerald Ridge as part of the illustrious Fortune family and one of the heirs to land that included a famed cattle ranch and a flourishing guest ranch and spa, Poppy had been blessed with an abundance of privilege. More importantly, she'd been shown unconditional love by her parents. In their happy marriage, she had an example of the best kind of relationship goals. Never mind that at thirty, she was nowhere close to establishing the family she knew would make her happy.

After a failed engagement and a string of less-than-successful relationships, Poppy was almost convinced that the white-picket-fence future she'd envisioned wasn't actually in the cards for her. And after all these years, one man still stood out in her mind and heart when she let herself go there.

Leo Leonetti—the one that got away.

They'd only dated a short time, but he remained the yardstick by which she measured her attraction to every other guy. Sadly, they all came up short and even more pathetic, the secret torch she still carried was for a guy who'd told her outright he didn't want a relationship. She'd moved on but the memory of how happy she'd felt with him still lingered.

That said, her doubts about finding her dream man didn't change the amount of love she held in her heart and wanted to give freely. Being a foster parent would allow her to make a difference in the world beyond the boundaries of the land on which she'd been born and raised.

She knew the role would offer challenges and potential heartbreak but was committed to doing her best. Her heart filled with the knowledge that she would create a safe and nurturing environment for whoever entered her house, just like she'd always had at her childhood home.

As her mother continued to stir the pot, the scent of earthy mushrooms and rich cream filled the kitchen. Her parents shared the massive house that anchored the ranch with her uncle Hayden and aunt Darla. The Fortune brothers of her father's generation living together had been a stipulation of her grandfather's will. Although her dad and uncle didn't always get along, they each managed to raise their respective three kids under the same roof.

There had been plenty of room for all of them, and the families had primarily lived in separate wings, distance keeping the arguments between the brothers somewhat at bay. It had only been in recent years that Poppy and her siblings had formed close relationships with their cousins. It started when her cousin Drake and brother Rafe developed the Gift of Fortune, an initiative sponsored by the family that allowed deserving recipients to be invited to the ranch for a complimentary week of pampering.

Her dad and uncle had become friendlier after Garth and Hayden retired from the daily running of the ranch, but the two older Fortune couples still mainly lived separate lives in the same house. Poppy appreciated that there were two big kitchens thanks to renovations her father and uncle had done years earlier. Her family typically used the kitchen original to the homestead, and she loved the vibe of the weathered beams that ran across the ceiling, the rich granite of the countertops, the professional-grade appliances her father had installed for his wife, along with distressed cabinets and a wide plank floor.

Even with state-of-the-art accessories, the kitchen had a homey feel, beckoning people to settle in for a cup of tea or a home-cooked meal at the round oak table that could easily seat ten. Poppy had modeled her own kitchen on this same aesthetic, albeit on a much smaller scale.

"I'll get bowls and toss the salad," she told her mother, getting up from the table.

"And grab champagne glasses from the dining room

while you're at it," Shelley added. "We're going to toast to your new role."

The doorbell rang at that moment. Both Poppy and her mother turned toward the unfamiliar sound. Fortune's Gold Ranch was an easy ten-minute drive from downtown Emerald Ridge, but most visitors went straight to the ranch office or the spa. It was rare to have people stop by the big house unannounced.

"Who'd drop in at supper time?" Shelley asked. She turned off the heat and covered the pot once more.

"No clue." Poppy headed toward the front of the house. "I'll go answer it."

The sun had already set, but darkness hadn't entirely swallowed up the last bit of the day's light, so she could see the outline of a woman through one of the windows flanking the tall front door. Poppy suppressed a groan as she got closer and made sure to "fix her face," as her mother would advise, before opening the door to greet Courtney Wellington, one of their closest neighbors and a fellow ranch owner in town.

"Hello, Courtney."

"I thought that was your Bronco in the driveway," the woman said by way of hello. "It's hard to miss."

Poppy looked past Courtney, who was dressed in bright pink slacks, a bedazzled T-shirt and a denim blazer. A distinctive outfit for Emerald Ridge, a town where most people wore casual or cowboy chic clothing. She smiled at her beloved Ladybug, as she'd named her bright red SUV. "Poppy red is my favorite color."

Courtney made a noncommittal sound. Her caterpillar-thick lashes lowered as she gave Poppy a quick once-over. "It's nice that something about you stands out. Is

your mother home? I suppose she is since you're here."
She offered a smile that reminded Poppy of a coyote
baring its teeth. "I'm surprised to see a youngish, single
girl like yourself hanging out at home on the weekend.
You certainly aren't going to attract a man that way."

Poppy blinked and forgot all about fixing her face.
She did her best to limit her interactions with the catty
blonde who had booked a full day at the spa shortly after
marrying her late husband. As the story went, Courtney and Mr. Wellington met in Dallas and had a whirl-
wind courtship that ended in marriage a mere month
after their first encounter. Most of the locals in Emerald Ridge assumed Courtney had been the pursuer in
the relationship, given that she'd been fresh off her second divorce when she met the wealthy rancher two decades her senior.

Like her mother, Poppy wanted to give people the
benefit of the doubt. However, on her first and only visit
to the spa, Courtney had left one of Poppy's best aestheticians in tears and skimped on tips for every one of her
service providers, loudly complaining between appoint-
ments about the quality of the facilities and products.

Fortune's Gold Ranch Spa was regularly featured on
the crème de la crème of luxury spa best-of lists in various high-end travel magazines. Their clients ranged
from devoted locals to A-list celebrities to the wives
of influential dignitaries as well as members of several
European royal families who liked the idea of being
pampered while experiencing a taste of what they might
consider the Wild West.

Poppy could handle the jabs Courtney threw, but she'd
never forgive the woman for dissing the spa staff.

She opened her mouth to offer a scathing comeback, but at that moment, she felt her mother's gentle hand on her shoulder.

"Hello, Courtney," Shelley said, her tone welcoming. "What brings you here tonight?"

"I was heading home from town, and since you'd mentioned that Garth was out of town until tomorrow, I figured I'd stop by for a friendly visit. You can be a bit of a homebody, Shelley."

Her mom's fingers gripped Poppy's shoulder when she would have lunged forward. Of course, Courtney didn't notice the effect her words were having on Poppy.

"I stopped by the liquor store," she continued, holding up one hand. Poppy hadn't noticed before that she had a bottle of white wine in it. "I thought we could have a drink to celebrate getting through January. I'm a bit restless with the short days and cooler temperatures. But now we have one winter month behind us. That calls for a toast."

"Actually, you can join the celebration we're having for my daughter," Shelley offered, stepping back and drawing Poppy with her so Courtney could enter the house.

She winked at Poppy as she entered. "I chose something from the Leonetti Vineyards. Didn't you date Leo at one point? Talk about a catch. That is one handsome hunk of a man. Too bad you couldn't keep him on the hook."

Poppy resisted the urge to stomp her foot. She didn't want Courtney anywhere near her, let alone crashing the celebratory dinner with her mother or reminding her of her past romantic failures.

"New job?" Courtney handed the wine to Poppy and then followed Shelley through the house, leaving Poppy to trail behind. "New boyfriend?" She chuckled as if she'd made some riotous joke.

"Poppy is going to be a foster parent." Shelley's voice was filled with pride, and an answering swell of it filled her heart. She loved the sound of that sentence.

"Wow," Courtney murmured. "That's really something."

Poppy forced a smile. "I'm excited to make a difference in the lives of children who temporarily need a stable home."

Her mom grabbed the bottle of champagne from the fridge, placed it on the counter and then disappeared into the dining room, where the crystal was kept.

"You must be okay with your nonexistent dating life," Courtney mused as she sat at one of the leather swivel chairs tucked under the overhang of the center island.

Once again, Poppy felt her mouth drop open. "I'm not sure one has anything to do with the other."

"Oh, yeah," Courtney retorted, reaching into her purse and pulling out her cell phone. "Because eligible single men are known to be into women with random kids hanging off them like barnacles."

There was a beat of silence while Shelley placed the glasses on the counter. She seemed as nonplussed as Poppy by their intrusive neighbor's rudeness.

"I mean, it's a selfless and admirable thing you're doing," Courtney quickly added as if realizing she'd gone too far. "Kudos to you for being a good person. That's something to celebrate."

"Thank you." Poppy had a hard time making her lips curve into another smile.

"Especially if your own biological clock isn't tick-tocking."

"Let's open the champagne," Shelley said.

"Three cheers for Saint Poppy," Courtney agreed, which didn't sound like a compliment. "Actually, I'm glad you're here." She reached into her purse again. "I was going to give these to your mother, but you can take a look for yourself."

"A look at…?" Poppy couldn't imagine wanting to see anything Courtney Wellington had to offer.

"Products from Annelise's skincare line, AW Glow-Care." Courtney set three small tubes on the counter. "These are sample sizes, of course, but you'll see the sublime quality after just one use. My stepdaughter is super talented. I told her the spa should carry her products and use them in all their services. It would be a big improvement over—"

She broke off when her phone began to ring. "Excuse me, I need to take this. Ranch owner business." Without batting an eye, Courtney accepted the call. "Hello? This is Mrs. Wellington…" She hopped off the chair with the phone at her ear and walked out of the kitchen. "Tell me exactly what you think I'm supposed to do about your problem."

Her words trailed off as she disappeared around the corner. Poppy allowed herself to both silently sympathize with whomever Courtney was reaming a new one and to feel a waterfall of relief that it wasn't her for a few minutes.

"She means well," Shelley offered with a wan smile.

Poppy burst out laughing. "So does a rattler when it strikes. The snake is just doing what snakes do."

Shelley rolled her lips together in an apparent attempt to keep from laughing as well, then popped the cork on the champagne. "You can't compare our closest neighbor to a venomous reptile."

"If the fangs fit," Poppy murmured as she unscrewed one of the lids from Annelise's sample tubes. She had no issue with either of Courtney's stepchildren. Jax was a year older than her and Annelise a few years younger. They hadn't run in the same circles, but she'd always gotten a good feeling about the other woman.

"I wonder why Annelise didn't come to you directly about her skincare line?" Shelley mused as she poured the bubbly liquid into the three flutes.

"Maybe because she isn't pushy and manipulative like some people I know." Poppy rubbed the thick cream into the back of her hand. "Wow. It smells amazing."

"Would you consider carrying the line at the spa?"

"Absolutely. We already source most of our products from Texas-based companies. Finding a quality line from a local business, especially one that's female-owned, would be even better. I'll call Annelise next week to set up a meeting to learn more about the ingredients and production. I like the idea of it."

"Maybe Courtney stopping by is a good thing after all," her mom remarked.

Poppy rolled her eyes.

"Why are ranch hands *so* difficult to deal with?" Courtney asked with an exasperated sigh as she returned to the kitchen. "Make sure to fill my glass to the rim, Shelley darling."

Courtney didn't seem to want or expect a response to most of her words. She was a woman who was clearly enamored with the sound of her own voice. Poppy exchanged a look with her mother and then moved toward the stove to scoop up a bowl of risotto. The doorbell rang again just as she grabbed a ladle from the utensil jar next to the stovetop.

"I'll get it." She dropped the ladle and hurried toward the front of the house. One visitor on a chilly winter night was odd enough, but two felt like some kind of sign. At least Poppy chose to take it as a sign that she would have an excuse not to focus on that awful woman.

But no one stood on the other side when she opened the door. Even odder. She glanced toward the darkness that had overtaken everything past the glow of the porch light and was about to close the door again when something made her look down.

"What the...?" A white wicker laundry basket sat on the porch. In it, wrapped in a pale blue blanket, was a baby.

Chapter Two

Poppy scooped up the basket, kicked the door closed with the heel of her boot and then rushed back toward the kitchen. She didn't want to shout and risk disturbing the sleeping infant. A newborn by the size of his tiny features. She assumed the baby was a boy based on the blue blanket and the little cotton cap with airplanes that fit snugly around his head.

"I started toasting without you," Courtney announced, holding her half-drank champagne flute.

Poppy ignored her. "Mom, call 911! Someone left a baby on the porch."

The two older women let out matching gasps of shock, and Poppy realized she was also having trouble catching her breath. She forced air in and out of her lungs as she set the basket on the kitchen table. She needed to keep her wits about her. This was no time to freak out, at least outwardly.

"Hello, sweetheart," she cooed to the baby as she unfolded the blanket. He wore a blue-footed one-piece, and her gaze snagged on the name crookedly embroidered on the front. "Your name is Joey," she told the baby as she lifted him from the basket.

"How did that thing get here?" Courtney demanded.

"He's a *baby*," Poppy said through gritted teeth. "I don't know how he ended up on your front porch." She could hear her mother, who had walked to the room's far end, speaking with the emergency services operator. "There was no one out there when I opened the door."

"An ambulance is on the way," Shelley reported as she lowered the phone and moved toward them. "Is he cold?"

Poppy shook her head, staring with wonder at the tiny form cradled in her arms. Joey's mouth worked for a few seconds, but he remained asleep.

Courtney backed away a few steps like Poppy held a porcupine. "I should go," she whispered to no one in particular, her voice hollow like she was in shock.

"There's a note," Poppy told her mother, pointing to the basket and ignoring Courtney.

Shelley picked up the piece of paper, the edges ragged like it had hastily been ripped from a notebook. "'This baby is a Fortune,'" Shelley read slowly, her eyes widening. "'Please care for him since I can't.'"

Courtney gasped again, the sound grating on Poppy's last nerve. "Some poor girl must have felt incredibly desperate to leave her baby on a stranger's porch. Although someone in this house apparently isn't a stranger to her."

Poppy's gut tightened at the implications of Courtney's words, then soured as she continued, "Which of your boys do you think is to blame? Or maybe one of your nephews?" Courtney gripped the phone in her hand more tightly. "Or…"

Poppy and Shelley both stared at the other woman.

"Or what?" Poppy demanded.

"A man can father a child well past his prime." Courtney shrugged when Shelley's mouth dropped open. "I'm just saying—"

"Weren't you *just saying* you need to go?" Poppy shifted so that the baby was no longer in Courtney's direct line of sight, the immediate surge of protectiveness she felt for the abandoned child almost overwhelming.

"I'll walk you out." Her mom gripped Courtney's elbow. "Please don't tell anyone about the baby until we have more information on him."

"Your secret is safe with me," Poppy heard Courtney promise as Shelley led her toward the front door.

"Whose secret *are* you, little man?" she asked the bundle in her arms when she was alone in the kitchen. As if responding to her voice, the baby blinked and stared up at her with the clearest blue-gray eyes she'd ever seen.

"You're safe now," she promised Joey like he could understand her. "Nothing and no one will hurt you while I'm around."

The baby drew a deep breath before his heavy eyelids drooped and closed again.

"The EMTs should be here soon," her mother said as she returned to Poppy's side. She studied the baby for a long moment, then rummaged through the basket. "A few diapers, a plastic bottle and a container of powder formula," she reported, then looked at her daughter with concern. "I don't understand this, Poppy."

"Me neither, Mom, but if I can get approval from social services, I'm going to take care of Joey until we figure it out." Her gaze drifted to the note on the table. "Do you really think—"

A pounding at the front door interrupted her question. Not that she needed to ask it out loud. Her mom had to be wondering the same thing as Poppy. Could one of her brothers, or *heaven forbid,* her father, be responsible for this baby? It was difficult to imagine a world where any of the men related to her would make a woman feel like she had no options other than to abandon a newborn.

The EMTs, a young woman with a thick braid and a gray-haired man, entered the kitchen. Poppy reluctantly handed over Joey and watched as they did an initial exam. According to the woman, whose badge identified her as Monica, his vitals were all in the normal range. Her partner was called Stan, and they were efficient in their care but not particularly loving—at least not enough for Poppy.

They also refused to allow her to ride to the county hospital in the ambulance with Joey, and as they left with him, longing split Poppy's chest, a burning physical ache.

She turned to her mother after closing the front door. "I'm going to the hospital."

"We need a family meeting," Shelley said simultaneously.

"Not until I make sure he's okay."

"The doctors and nurses will take care of him."

"Not like I can." Poppy reached for her mother's hands and squeezed. "I don't understand this any more than you, but the fact that he was left on your doorstep the night after I received my approval is a sign, Mom. I'm supposed to be a part of Joey's life, at least temporarily."

Shelley looked like she wanted to argue, and Poppy understood the fear she saw in her mother's blue eyes. The mystery of the identity of Joey's mother and father would eventually be solved, but whatever they discovered could rock the Emerald Ridge Fortune family to its core.

Still, nothing was more important at this point than the baby.

She'd once dreamed of having her own baby, and maybe she'd even imagined a child with Leo Leonetti's soulful brown eyes. But she'd given up that girlish fantasy along with her belief in true love yet knew caring for a baby who needed someone was the kind of love she could offer in spades.

"Keep me updated." Shelley pulled her in for a long hug. "I'll call your father and uncle and let them know what's happened. The EMTs said the police would also come to the house to investigate. We'll figure out where Joey belongs sooner than later."

Poppy nodded, and after grabbing her purse and jacket from the coat rack near the front door, she hurried to her car. County Hospital was a twenty-minute drive from the ranch, but she had every intention of making it in fifteen. On the way, she would call her caseworker to start the process of being designated as the child's foster parent if he needed someone. Despite her mother's words, Poppy had the strangest feeling that the place sweet Joey belonged was with her.

Across town, Leo Leonetti drained his wineglass and then immediately regretted his hasty swallow. Or, more specifically, he rued his promise to himself to enjoy only one glass of wine with dinner each night.

As one of the owners and CEO of Leonetti Vineyards, the oldest and most prestigious winery in Texas,

Leo had an entire cellar of exceptional varietals. He allowed himself to imbibe more freely on a special occasion or the rare instance when he led a personal tour of his family's operations.

But typically, one glass suited his taste and personality.

"You're thirty-four, Leonardo," his grandfather Enzo reminded him as if Leo might have forgotten his age. "A man in his prime should have a wife and family. You don't want to end up a shriveled raisin trying to chase little ones through the grapes."

"Papa, I don't think I'll be hitting raisin status anytime soon." Leo twirled the stem of the empty glass between two fingers. "For now, the grapes *are* my children."

Leo had been at the helm of the vineyard for nearly ten years since his father's death from a fatal heart attack, a shocking loss that still left an ache in his soul. Leo had been in the Alps, indulging his love of travel and new adventures, when the call came from his mother.

All that wanderlust had been snuffed out in an instant, and he'd returned to Texas to take his place as a steward of the land his family had owned for generations.

He loved everything about the process of making wine, and under his leadership, the vineyard and winery were thriving. His younger sisters, Bella, Antonia and Gia, were equal partners in running the operation. While Enzo and Leo's mother, Martina, had retired from any formal role in the business, Leo appreciated having them close for guidance and support.

More recently, it became his turn to support Enzo. His grandfather, who enjoyed splitting his time between

Emerald Ridge and Italy, had been diagnosed a few years ago with stage-three liver cancer.

Although the first round of chemo and radiation had taken a toll on the eighty-two-year-old man, they also believed the treatments had driven the insidious disease into remission.

Just before Christmas, Enzo had called a family meeting and shared that the cancer had returned. The proud and stubborn man had initially planned to forgo additional medical interventions to concentrate on enjoying his life and whatever time he had left with his family.

However, with encouragement from Leo, his mom and sisters, Enzo had decided on another round of treatment, determined to kick cancer's butt one more time. Leo had been grateful to the point of tears, unable to imagine the vineyard or their family without his larger-than-life grandfather. And he knew enough now to appreciate every precious moment they had together.

Other than the moments where he was being lectured on settling down. He might not have a wife—or girlfriend—but he wasn't exaggerating when he said his most intense relationship was with his work. His grandfather remained strong and in good spirits, but there was no guarantee how long that would last. Leo wanted to continue building on the success of Leonetti Vineyards so that Enzo would know his legacy was in good hands.

"Grapes will not keep you warm at night." Enzo shook his head. "They will not celebrate your joys and comfort you in times of sorrow. My beautiful Ella was the light of my life for many years, Leo. I only want that same thing for you."

Leo's grandparents had enjoyed the most picture-

MICHELLE MAJOR   25

perfect relationship he could imagine, a flawless match in every way, until his grandmother's death in a tragic car accident when Leo was a boy. However, it hadn't been the same with his own parents. His father had loved his mother and been a devoted parent, if sometimes harsh and impatient.

Franco hadn't loved the vineyard the way Enzo did. The way *Leo* did, even when he felt the weight of responsibility he carried like a boulder on his back.

How could he settle down with a woman, and even more so, a family, when he knew he could never live up to the example his nana and papa set?

Maybe if his parents hadn't been rushed into marriage, thanks to a surprise pregnancy, his dad could have taken more time to figure out who he was and who he wanted to be in the world. Leo couldn't imagine balancing his focus on both work and a romantic relationship. He'd have to potentially sacrifice one or both parts of his life due to what was expected of him within the family business and the demands a relationship might put on him.

Suddenly a vision of Poppy Fortune with her blond hair and gentle green eyes appeared in his mind. She'd been the one woman who'd ever made him want to reconsider his refusal to open his heart.

If he was being honest, the time they'd dated had been the best and worst of his life. The best because spending time with Poppy felt like being bathed in sunshine on the most perfect summer day. She was beautiful, smart, funny and made him practically forget his own name because he'd been so infatuated with her.

Which had led to the worst part. The idea of losing control of his emotions had terrified Leo, leading him to spew out some verbal garbage about how he had no intention of settling down or getting serious with one woman. On their third date. It was like he'd shoved his own foot straight down his throat. And Poppy had dumped him like a sack of rotten potatoes in return.

He'd deserved it and that moment proved that Leo wasn't equipped to succeed at both love and work. With the pressure of generations of Leonettis on his shoulders, failing at the vineyard wasn't an option. Maybe his father had understood that, and the pressure had taken a toll until his heart couldn't withstand it.

"I'll get there, Papa," he promised, even though he had no idea if that was true.

Enzo stabbed a piece of plump gnocchi and popped it into his mouth, chewing with gusto as he stared at his grandson. Martina had made dinner before she and Leo's sisters left for their monthly book club meeting. "You can't keep hiding in the rows of vines, my boy. You are no longer a child, and this isn't a game. There's a time for everything, but time is finite. I want to see you happy."

Leo's throat burned. He could tell by the color rising in his grandfather's cheeks that this conversation upset the old man.

He hated not being able to offer the reassurance his grandfather wanted. "I'm happy, Papa. Work makes me happy. Spending time with you makes me happy." Another glass of wine would make him happy.

"Nothing makes a man happier than love," Enzo insisted.

Leo couldn't argue because he wasn't sure he'd ever been in love. He didn't know if he was even capable of feeling that depth of emotion for another person. Maybe he'd inherited the trait from his father and that inability to love had contributed to Franco's discontent. Leo might have been able to fall in love with Poppy if he'd let himself, but he wouldn't. He couldn't. All he knew for sure was that he wasn't enough to be the man his grandpa saw in him.

He forced a smile and sopped up a generous amount of oil with a piece of the crusty bread his mother had baked earlier. "Valentine's Day is right around the corner," he said with a lightness he didn't feel. "Who knows what might happen?"

But Leo knew. He had more work on his plate than he could handle in a month of eighty-hour work weeks. There was no time for romance, even if he was interested in it. Which he wasn't.

Still, if it made Enzo happy, Leo would pretend. Wasn't that what his father had done as well? Smooth the waters and pretend like everything was okay.

Enzo let out a raspy sigh. "You speak the right words, my boy, but your heart isn't in them." The older man held up a hand when Leo would've argued. "But now you've put it out there, and it's up to fate to pick up your challenge. Love can happen in an instant. That was how it was with your grandmother and me on our family's trip to Italy when I was only sixteen. I saw her, and everything else fell away. She was the answer to a question I didn't even know enough to ask. If it can happen to me…"

"A toast to Nana, rest her soul." Leo held up his water glass, and Enzo clinked it with his wine goblet.

"To my darling Ella."

"Tell me again about your courtship with Nana and how you swept her off her feet."

Enzo's features relaxed as he smiled and sat back in his chair. He never tired of speaking about his wife. The memories, bittersweet as they must be in some ways, always put him in a good mood.

Leo took another bite of the potato pasta and settled into his chair. He would much rather hear about his grandparents' beautiful love story than think about the work involved to create one of his own.

That was work he had no intention of pursuing in the near future.

Chapter Three

Leo finished his run at his mother's front porch the next morning. He wanted to check in on Enzo after their dinner last night.

Sleep had been elusive as he'd been plagued with dreams of driving his truck down a washed-out dirt road to reach his family, but the wheels continually got stuck in ruts. Did the frustrating dream have anything to do with his guilt over not being able to give his grandfather what the older man wanted?

Enzo hadn't pushed any further about Leo settling down once he'd started reminiscing about his own love story. Still, Leo couldn't shake the nagging sense that his unwillingness to get on board the dating train made him a disappointment to the man who meant the most to him in the world.

Truth be told, he was a regular passenger on the dating train but only for short-term trips. He loved everything about women—the way they looked and smelled, how their bodies were soft in places his was hard. He'd never had any complaints in the bedroom department, and he kept their expectations in check as far as what he could and couldn't offer.

Usually, his dates cut him more slack than he deserved, thanks to his charm. It wouldn't be an exaggeration to say that Leo had charisma for days. But Poppy Fortune had seemed to look directly into his soul, bypassing his megawatt smile and twinkling brown eyes, and found him lacking in all the ways that counted.

Leo used the hem of his T-shirt to wipe the sweat off his brow as he took the front porch steps two at a time. Why was he thinking of Poppy so much lately? He'd dated plenty of women since, and no one cared about his inability to commit. Not when he was so damn much fun, or so he'd been told.

His papa, who'd also seen through Leo's attempt to sweet-talk his way out of answering difficult questions, would probably appreciate Poppy. She'd been a straight shooter in addition to being gorgeous, but Leo hadn't had more than a chance encounter with her in half a decade.

Emerald Ridge might be a small town, but it was easy enough to avoid a person who, with one glance, could make him uncomfortably aware of the ways he came up short.

He reached for the door the same time his mother opened it, her eyes red-rimmed and her lips turned down into a trembling frown.

"Mom, what's wrong?" He reached out and gripped her arm. "Is it Papa?"

Martina closed her eyes as she nodded. "He started having trouble breathing at about four this morning. We couldn't get his oxygen levels right, so I called 911. He argued with me, saying he was fine but looked real bad, Leo. They took him to the hospital twenty minutes ago."

"Why didn't you call me?" he demanded, his mind reeling. "Are Bella, Antonia and Gia there?"

"Not yet." His mom stepped forward, and Leo wrapped his arms around her. Enzo had moved into one of the guest rooms in the main house after his most recent diagnosis. His grandfather balked at being coddled and didn't want to be a burden for his daughter-in-law, but Martina had insisted.

It gave Leo a measure of relief to know his mom was there if Enzo needed anything, but he tried to stop by at least once a day to give her a break. His sisters did the same, and in some ways, their grandfather's illness had brought the four of them even closer. It was truly life-changing to deal with the mortality of a loved one.

"He made me promise not to wake any of you." Martina leaned back and looked up into his face, her gentle eyes filling with tears. "I knew you'd be by this morning because you're such a good son and grandson."

Was he? "What do they think caused the breathing issues?" Leo asked softly. He couldn't help but think it might have to do with his grandfather's agitation during their dinner conversation last night.

His mom shook her head. "They don't know. I'm going to shower and head to the hospital. The doctor called a few minutes ago and said Enzo is stable but weak. He doesn't think this is…" She placed a hand to her mouth and stifled a sob.

"It's going to be okay, Mom. I'll head there now." He turned away then paused as he realized he'd have to jog back to his house, which was only a quarter mile away on the fifty acres the vineyard encompassed, but it felt too far.

"Take the field truck," his mother suggested, nodding toward the storage barn. "The keys are inside."

Leo nodded. "I'll see you there."

By the time he exited the elevator on the third floor, his mind was a jumble of regret and worry. Martina would never accuse him, but how could it be a coincidence that Enzo had suffered this sort of setback after the conversation with Leo?

He spoke with the nurse at the desk, who gave him a strange look before asking if he'd run the whole way to the hospital in the wind. Leo quickly smoothed a hand over his rumpled hair—he'd been pulling at the ends for most of the drive over, a nervous habit he couldn't seem to break. "I came as soon as I heard my grandfather was here," he explained.

The woman's gaze became more understanding. "Your grandpa is sleeping, but he's stable. The morning took a lot out of him. Rest is the best thing right now."

"Can I see him?" Leo didn't bother to hide the desperation in his voice.

She looked like she wanted to deny him, but eventually nodded. "Room 301, down the hall to your right. You can stop in, but please don't wake him. His body is dealing with a lot."

"I know. Thank you." The words came out a croak as the ball of emotion in his throat threatened to overtake him.

He glanced at his watch as he headed toward Enzo's room. His mom would have called his sisters by now, and they'd be there soon. He didn't want to see or speak to anyone until he got his emotions under control.

Leo liked being in control, and he felt the opposite of

that as he studied his grandfather asleep in the hospital room, the machine next to him displaying his vital signs.

Enzo's eyes were closed and his once-broad chest rose and fell in what looked like labored breaths. Clear tubes led from a tank to his nose, supplying the oxygen he couldn't seem to take in on his own. Because of his explicit instructions, there would be no CPR performed if his breathing stopped, which meant that Enzo had to recover on his own.

Although Leo was at loss for how to help, he'd find a way. He would not lose another man he loved…not yet.

His stomach grumbled loudly and he backed out of the room. Like his grandfather, he was a three-square-meals-a-day kind of guy and didn't function well in the morning before coffee or breakfast.

Now that he'd seen for himself that Enzo was stable, his earlier adrenaline rush began to wear off. He thanked the woman at the nurse's station again, then took the stairs at the end of the hall to the first-floor cafeteria.

He wasn't ready to go home and shower, but some food and caffeine might help clear his head. After paying for the coffee and an egg-and-chorizo burrito, he headed to the two-person tables in front of the bank of windows that looked out over the hospital parking lot then did a double take as he recognized the woman sitting nearby.

"Poppy?"

Poppy Fortune, staring out the window, looked up at Leo with those big sea-foam-green eyes that had captivated him when they'd first met.

Her mouth formed a small O before she flashed a self-conscious smile. "Hey, Leo, this is a surprise." She ran a hand through her shiny blond hair, which fell nearly to the middle of her back. It had been shoulder-length when they'd gone on their few memorable dates. "I didn't expect to see anyone I knew here."

"Me neither," he agreed, resisting the urge to lift his arm and take a sniff under it. Maybe he should have made time to shower after all. "Is everything okay?"

She took a few seconds to respond as if uncertain how to answer. "It will be. I'll make sure of it."

That piqued his curiosity. "Anything I can help with?"

The question prompted a choked laugh from her. "Definitely not. What about you?" She glanced behind him like she was looking for his mom or one of his sisters. "I hope you aren't here because of your grandfather."

Leo's grip tightened on the coffee cup. Of course, most people in Emerald Ridge knew about Enzo and his cancer battle. If memory served, Shelley Fortune had delivered a home-cooked meal or two during the months Leo's mother cared for Enzo during chemo and radiation. "He had trouble breathing early this morning, so he's been admitted until that's under control."

"Oh, no! Sorry to hear that." Poppy reached out and squeezed his arm. "I'll keep him in my prayers and hope for a fast recovery. Your grandfather is quite a character."

Leo wasn't prepared for the wave of emotion her touch elicited from him and gave a sharp nod. "He is that. I should eat so I can get back up there." For some reason, he didn't want to walk away but...

"Would you like to join me?" She gestured to the empty chair across from her. "I've been here all night, so fair warning, I might not be great company."

"I can't imagine an instance when you aren't great

company," Leo told her as he sat down. "Not to pry, but your reason for being here was cryptic. Care to elaborate?"

She stared at him for so long he wondered if she'd fallen asleep with her eyes open. "I suppose a situation like the one I'm in won't stay quiet around here. Not for long."

The little hairs on the back of his neck rose to attention. "What kind of situation?"

She took a breath and said quietly, "A baby was left on my parents' doorstep last night."

Midbite of burrito, Leo nearly spit the thing across the table at her. "Say *what*?"

The words came out louder than he meant, and after making sure no one had overheard him, she continued, "Keep your voice down, please."

"Sorry, you just caught me off guard," he said quietly. "Whose baby is it?"

"We don't know. His name is Joey, and according to the note left with him, his father is a Fortune."

"One of the FGR Fortunes?" Leo's mind was racing, and it had nothing to do with the half cup of coffee he'd gulped down a few minutes earlier.

Poppy shrugged and looked down at her phone. Suddenly, the pallor of her complexion and the tight line of her lips took on a different meaning. He could tell she was not only exhausted but worried, both about the baby and what this could mean for her family.

"Neither of my brothers or cousins believe he could be theirs. No one is claiming him." She squeezed shut her eyes briefly then raised her gaze to Leo's. "Except me."

"You?" He placed the burrito back on the plate, his hunger wholly forgotten.

"A caseworker I've grown close to at social services helped me get assigned as his foster parent right away." She touched her phone's home screen then lifted it in Leo's direction. "This is Joey. The pediatrician on call wanted him to stay the night to be monitored. They don't think he's more than a few days old. But I'm taking him home as soon as he's discharged."

Leo looked at the photo of the infant swaddled like a baby burrito and sleeping soundly. His heart turned over uncomfortably. "For how long?"

"As long as he needs me," she said, almost defensively.

"Don't you have to be certified or something to foster a kid, let alone an infant?"

"I am." Her eyes blazed with flecks of gold as if daring him to challenge her. "I've been through all the training and background checks and received my final approval this week. Just in time to give this sweet baby a home."

"You're a foster mom," he murmured. "You decided to do this on your own?"

She bristled. "No doubt you heard that Michael and I called things off."

"Yeah. Bella mentioned it. He always seemed like a tool to me, so good riddance on that count."

Poppy laughed, covering her mouth to stifle it. "Only you could find a way to lighten the mood at a time like this, Leo."

He wasn't sure if it was meant as a compliment, but he damn sure intended to take it as one.

"Do you think I can't handle this by myself?" Her smile faded.

"I think you can do whatever you set your mind to." He lifted the coffee cup to his lips then lowered it again. "I admire the hell out of you for it, Poppy. That baby is lucky to have you, and so is your family, whether or not one of the Fortune guys is responsible."

Poppy bit down on her lower lip as a tear fell from the corner of one eye. She dashed it away and offered him a watery smile. "I wasn't expecting that."

Leo was horrified. He hated to see any woman crying.

"But thank you," she told him. "It means a lot, especially coming from you."

He lifted a brow. "Why coming from me?"

"Your feelings about commitment were abundantly clear and…" She made a face. "From how the ladies talk at the spa, your stance hasn't changed."

"The ladies talk about me? That's scary as hell." He leaned in closer, curiosity piqued. "Wait. Do *you* talk about me, Poppy?"

She huffed out a laugh. "Not to disappoint, Leo, but I have more important things to think *and* talk about than you."

Ouch. "That's fair," he conceded. "Especially now."

"To be honest," she told him with a grimace, "I'm not sure I fully grasped the responsibility I was signing up for as a foster parent until my caseworker approved me as Joey's guardian. Being in charge of such a helpless baby is intimidating to say the least. Things in real life feel a lot more…" She shrugged again. "It's a lot of responsibility."

Leo forced himself to concentrate on what she was saying, even though his thoughts snagged on the comment about his reputation.

He supposed he shouldn't be surprised that women around town gossiped about him and his unwillingness to commit. He also should have guessed his grandfather wouldn't be so easily swayed by his vague promises of eventually settling down.

Poppy's phone vibrated, and she quickly pushed back from the table. "Joey is being discharged," she said, looking both excited and nervous. "Here I go. Wish me luck."

"You don't need luck." Leo also stood. "You're going to be fantastic at this. I hope everything works out for that baby, although there's no doubt it will with you in his corner."

"I hope your grandfather feels better soon." To his surprise, she leaned in and gave him a tight hug.

Her sweet scent and the feel of her curves pressed against him jumbled his brain, not to mention other parts of his body. Where the hell had that reaction come from?

He also wished he'd changed out of his workout clothes almost as much as he wished he could hold on to Poppy for longer, but she released him a second later. "Your family is lucky to have you as well, Leo. You're a fine man. Better than you give yourself credit for."

She hurried away before he could respond, which was a blessing because he had no idea what to say. Poppy was such a good person. They were practically strangers at this point. Yet in the midst of dealing with something highly overwhelming in her own life, she'd managed to make Leo feel better about himself than he had in a long time.

If Poppy believed he was a better man, maybe he could become one. If not for himself, then for his grandfather. There was no doubt Enzo would like her. Leo certainly did.

Even though she'd broken up with him, there were no hard feelings. In fact, seeing her again made him remember how drawn he'd been to her. He wanted to see her succeed in this foster care venture.

As he tossed the remainder of his burrito and the empty coffee cup into the trash on his way out of the cafeteria, he realized, to his surprise, he not only wanted her to succeed—he wanted to *help* her succeed. And he knew a way that might benefit them both.

It was ridiculous and far-fetched and would put him galaxies away from his comfort zone. But it also might make his grandpa happy and relieve some of the pressure Leo felt from the women in his family, who wanted him to settle down as much as Enzo did. The more he thought about his potential solution, the more he thought it might work. All he needed was to convince Poppy to agree. How hard could that be?

Chapter Four

Poppy wanted to cry as she swept up the last shards of her shattered coffeepot, her nerves and resolve feeling just as ruined.

She could hear Joey, who she'd put down in his crib only moments before, crying through the video monitor on the counter.

After checking the time, she left the dustpan on the counter and hurried toward the spare bedroom, where she'd spent most of the night with the baby in her arms.

Joey had barely made a peep from the time Poppy found him on her parents' front porch to his day in the hospital to the errands they'd run yesterday for the items she'd need to care for a newborn baby.

Instead of asking her mother or one of her brothers to watch him, she'd taken him with her, because the child was her responsibility.

Not theirs.

She'd also driven past the shops in Emerald Ridge's downtown and headed to the next town over so the busy-bodies and lookie-loos wouldn't have her family's private business to discuss. At least not while she was right in front of them.

Her mother had invited her to dinner last night. Although Poppy had declined that invitation, she couldn't deny Shelley's request that she attend a mandatory family meeting with both sets of the Fortune cousins this morning at the main house.

She hadn't expected to sleep well with everything on her mind, but she'd expected to sleep more than an hour. Unfortunately, Joey had started fussing about an hour after she'd put him down.

Neither of them had enjoyed a restful night. Between rocking him, feeding him, checking for whether his diaper needed changing and swaddling him in hopes that he might finally settle, Poppy had scoured the internet searching for tips on the care of infants. She knew as a foster parent, she would be looking after children that ranged in age and experience, but this was trial by fire for her first case, and already she felt a little singed.

She'd knocked the coffeepot off the counter before pouring a drop into her cup, which had been the cherry on the top of her crap sundae. There was no time to make another cup, but she knew she could get some liquid sustenance at her parents' house.

Hopefully, her family wouldn't see how much she was already failing at her role as a foster mom. If she had a husband and kids of her own, she might be experienced enough to know how to soothe a fussy baby.

Her mom would be able to tell her, but Poppy hated the thought of revealing even to Shelley how ill-equipped she felt for the job she wanted to succeed at more than anything.

The doorbell rang as she carried the still-fussy baby from the bedroom as her rescue mutt, Humphrey, gave a woof of welcome and trotted to the door. Maybe it was one of her brothers. They lived in houses similar to Poppy's in the same area on the ranch. Each of the Fortunes of her generation had homes built on the ranch when they'd been ready to leave the main house.

All of the lots consisted of five acres, which meant she had privacy while still being close enough to feel like they had a small cousin community. She bounced Joey gently in her arms as she padded to the door.

Hopefully, it was Rafe and not Shane. Her older brother might not want anything to do with kids after losing his wife and daughter in a tragic car accident, but at least he had experience with babies.

Except Leo Leonetti, not her brothers, stood smiling at her on the other side of the door. Instead of the sweaty workout garb he'd worn at the hospital, he looked crisp and dapper in dark gray pressed pants and a white button-down that contrasted in a toe-curling way with his olive-toned skin. Yesterday, she'd wanted to smooth her hand through his finger-tousled hair, but today, not one strand on the man's dark head was out of place.

She'd purposely avoided looking in the mirror this morning but could imagine what he saw as he studied her face after two sleepless nights. He didn't give any indication if he thought she looked as bad as she felt. Instead, he bent to scratch Humphrey behind the ears when the dog head-butted his leg.

Then, to her eternal gratitude, he held up a steaming cup of coffee from the local shop in town. "I asked if you had a standing order, and they said sugar-free caramel latte. I hope you haven't already had your fill of caffeine this morning."

Once again, Poppy was brought to the verge of tears in front of Leo, the last man on earth she wanted to see her cry.

"Yes, please, coffee." She adjusted her hold on Joey, who was still whimpering, and stepped back. "You are my hero."

Leo startled at the comment. "I highly doubt that. You look like you're on your way out. I hope I'm not here at a bad time."

"My mom called a family meeting to discuss the situation with Joey." She glanced at her watch again. "I've got a few minutes until we're supposed to be there but planned to leave early because my coffeepot had an unfortunate meet with the tile floor this morning. But now that you've saved me, I'm good."

"And how's the baby?" Leo asked, eyeing Joey somewhat dubiously.

"I don't think he likes me," Poppy admitted thickly.

"I doubt that."

She swallowed, then said, "Despite my training, taking care of a baby in real life is way more of a challenge than I realized. Pretty sure Joey knows I'm in over my head."

Leo's jaw tightened as he studied her. Why had she admitted the worry that picked at the edge of her deepest fear about herself to this man? He undoubtedly had no interest in hearing about her troubles.

"Why are you here?" she blurted, too frazzled and sleep-deprived to care whether or not she sounded rude.

Leo smiled. "In addition to my sixth sense about when someone needs a coffee fix, I have a proposition for you." To Poppy's surprise, he looked almost nervous saying the words.

"Do I look like a woman who's in the market to be propositioned?"

For whatever reason that seemed to drain some of the tension from his body.

"Maybe you'll be willing to entertain my idea because it also has to do with Joey. Our conversation in the hospital yesterday got me thinking about my contribution to the world and what's expected of me."

She quirked a brow. "Beyond running your family's vineyard and helping to care for your grandfather?"

Leo might not be willing to commit to a woman, but he wasn't precisely irresponsible in the rest of his life. She knew how much the winery had expanded under his leadership. His mom and sisters and almost every woman Poppy could name adored him.

"More specifically, the *expectation* my grandfather has for me. He wants me to settle down, and we had a somewhat heated conversation about it the night before he had his setback."

Joey quieted like he was listening intently to Leo's words. He had a great voice, deep and soothing and just a touch gravelly.

"Any update on your grandfather?" she asked, trying not to get sidetracked by Leo's handsomeness or his voice or how good he smelled—like clean laundry and some kind of male spice she couldn't name.

"He hasn't woken up enough for us to talk to him, but the doctors say he's stable, so that's good." Leo cleared his throat. "When he does, I want him to know that he doesn't have to worry about me or my stability or how I'm going to honor his legacy."

Her heart pinched at the pain in his voice.

"You aren't alone at the vineyard," she reminded Leo gently. "Your sisters have just as much invested in the Leonetti legacy that you do. It's not fully on your shoulders, capable as they might be."

His jaw tightened again, and his shoulders went ramrod stiff. "My grandfather... The point is, I don't know how much time we have with him, and I don't want to give him any reason to worry."

"I get that." Poppy nodded. "But what does that have to do with Joey and me?"

"I'd like to help you take care of him."

She started to laugh because he had to be joking then stopped herself. His expression was completely serious, earnest even.

"If I have zero experience caring for a baby, then I would guess you have less than zero."

He shot her an affronted look. "I'm a great uncle to Antonia's baby, or at least I will be when she's old enough to appreciate me."

"I don't doubt it. You'll be the perfect fun uncle. But have you changed a diaper?" she challenged.

"I watched a video on YouTube," Leo said without missing a beat. "The most important thing with a boy is that you cover everything while cleaning them so you don't get sprayed in the face."

Poppy had to admit she was impressed and also *had* been sprayed in the face last night. One more moment that added insult to injury. Leo Leonetti, a confirmed bachelor who avoided commitment at all costs, had the forethought to educate himself on diaper changing. Her foster parent classes had handled a lot. She was certified in infant CPR but had still managed to be sprayed in the face.

Joey squirmed in her arms and let out a wail, and she began to rock him back and forth in a vain attempt to quiet him.

"Okay. Let's cut to the chase. What exactly are you proposing here, Leo?"

"I want to co-parent Joey with you. I could even stay here if that would help."

He held up a hand when she would have argued. "Give me a chance, Poppy. I'll help out in whatever way you need. It would mean a lot to me, but not because you can't do it alone. I think it would mean a lot to my grandfather."

Poppy's heart pounded, and her limbs felt heavy. How could she handle everything that was expected of her right now and cope with her overwhelming exhaustion at the same time? Of course, she'd figure out a way. It's what mothers—and in her case, foster mothers—did. She didn't want Leo or anyone to think she couldn't handle this because she could. There was no doubt in her mind she would take care of Joey, but would she always feel this tired?

Stifling a yawn, she managed a smile. "I need to get to the family meeting."

Leo nodded. Disappointment flashed in his eyes but he took a step away. Joey continued to cry. "What if we did a test run?"

She frowned at him. "Like a test drive of a car?"

He shook his head. "No, like you give me a chance to prove I can handle helping with Joey. I know you have no reason to trust me, Poppy."

Yet somehow she believed she could, not that she was going to admit as much to him in this moment.

"I can watch Joey while you go to the meeting. You'll be close if we need anything, and I'd really like to help you."

"I'm not sure this is a good idea, Leo. Knowing how much everyone in my family talks, I could be at my parents' for a couple of hours."

"Take as long as you need. I'll call the office and tell them I won't be in until lunchtime."

She knew Joey would have a better chance of actually taking a nap if he was at her quiet house versus in the middle of what would undoubtedly be an emotional and loud scene at her parents'. Nerves flickered through her at the idea of letting someone else watch over the baby, but she couldn't deny that Leo's offer would make the morning a lot easier.

"Are you sure?" She searched his dark gaze for any sign of reluctance, but he looked relieved that she was considering his offer.

He reached for Joey and plucked him out of her arms like it was the most natural thing in the world. "I've got this, Poppy. I promise I won't let you down."

"Thank you," Poppy said, surprised both to find herself agreeing and also that, so far, Leo had offered her the most support with Joey. Not that her mother wouldn't if she asked. But Shelley was distracted, worrying about who might be revealed as Joey's father.

"Thanks for giving me a chance," Leo said as she picked up her purse from the kitchen table.

It felt like he knew she didn't trust his resolve to see through his sudden willingness to help. She didn't and fully expected to return to her house and never see Leo again after today—at least until they ran into each other in town.

But he was bailing her out at a precious moment, and she appreciated it.

He didn't bat an eye as she reviewed Joey's feeding and nap schedule, not that the baby was currently following any set schedule.

"Are you sure about this?" she asked one more time before heading to the meeting.

Leo flashed a smile so sincere it made her weak in the knees. *Get a hold of yourself*, she ordered.

"We'll be fine," he promised, then ran a hand over the top of Humphrey's furry head. "I've got my trusty helper, too."

Her dog pressed closer to Leo's side. She wasn't the only one susceptible to the man's charms.

"Call if you need anything. I can be back here in minutes."

"Take your time." Leo's smile widened. "Trust me, Poppy."

Sure. Trust a man who strolled back into her life like offering to raise a baby was no biggie.

Still, she appreciated the time this gave her. And if nothing else, it would make clear that Leo was not interested in getting involved with her and Joey the way he claimed. Better to find that out now before she let herself rely on him. This morning would prove something to them both.

Two hours later, Poppy reached for her car door handle. She wanted to blame her trembling fingers on too much caffeine and not enough food in her belly, even though she knew her muddled emotions caused it. Her mom and aunt Darla put out quite the spread for breakfast, and her brothers and cousins had dug in with gusto as they talked and argued about what Joey's appearance on the doorstep and the accompanying note would mean for the family.

Poppy hadn't been able to eat a thing. Trying to balance the upset she felt over the way they discussed Joey—like he was an unwanted overnight package delivered to the wrong address—with the understanding that the rests of her relatives were as confounded by the mystery surrounding him as her, and everyone processed that shock in their own way.

"Poppy."

She turned at the sound of her cousin's voice. Although her long blond hair was pulled back into a high ponytail and she wore scuffed boots, faded jeans and a denim shirt, Vivienne looked more like a ranch-style fashion influencer than the forewoman of the entire FGR cattle operation.

She jogged a few yards from the porch to Poppy's parked car and hugged her. "How are you really? We talked about a lot of things during that meeting, but none of them were the fact that you've been the one to step forward in such a huge way to care for that baby."

Tears pricked the back of Poppy's eyes. She really needed to eat something and get a hold of herself. One night caring for the boy and she was wearing her heart on her sleeve. "I'm fine and grateful my approval as a foster parent came through in time for me to provide a safe haven for Joey."

She looked past her cousin to the Texas hill country–style mansion that still felt like home to her even after years of living in her cozy house on the property. "This isn't his fault," she said quietly. "I'm not sure people are keeping that at the forefront of their minds. He's innocent."

Vivienne squeezed her arms and nodded. "They know, but when we all get together, it's a lot of Fortune energy in one room and emotions are running high. The DNA tests will prove that no one in my immediate family or yours is involved. That will make things easier."

Poppy didn't argue with her cousin, although she wasn't sure she agreed. Even if the results proved none of the Fortune men had fathered Joey, it wouldn't change the fact that he'd been left on their doorstep for a reason. She wanted to get to the bottom of that mystery no matter who his parents turned out to be.

"I hope you're right," she said.

"We've got your back, Pop, so if you need anything, just holler."

"That means the world to me," she told her cousin. Even though she knew Vivienne meant the words, Poppy felt a strange sort of protectiveness toward Joey, like she wanted to keep him safe from judgment even if he was too young to know it was happening. "I should get back to him," she said. "Thanks for checking on me, Viv."

The other woman started to take a step away, then paused. "You know you could have brought him to the meeting. My mom would have been thrilled."

Poppy nodded. Her Aunt Darla had been the only one to seem disappointed when Poppy had walked in without a baby in her arms.

"He didn't sleep well last night." She repeated the excuse she'd given her family for why Joey wasn't with her. Her parents had glanced at each other with visible relief, and Poppy had tried not to feel a pang of disappointment.

"Did someone from the spa daycare come over to watch him?" Vivienne asked. Poppy's staff was loyal to a fault and would help out in any way she needed, so it was a logical assumption, but she shook her head.

"No, I didn't want to get anyone from the spa involved before all of us met. The gossip will spread through town quickly enough. Better to keep things quiet for now."

"So who stayed with him?"

Poppy thought about ignoring the question, but that would only make her cousin more curious.

"I ran into an old friend at the hospital yesterday," she said, doing her best to sound casual. "Leo Leonetti was there visiting his grandfather."

"I didn't realize Enzo was back in the hospital," Vivienne said as her delicate brows drew together. "I thought his cancer treatments were going well."

"I don't know the details…" And what she did know wasn't hers to share. "But he's back home now."

"Which of the Leonetti sisters is watching him. My guess is Bella because—"

"Leo offered to help with Joey," Poppy interrupted. "I took him up on it."

Vivienne's jaw dropped. "The same Leo Leonetti who avoids any type of commitment that doesn't have to do with winemaking like he's sidestepping a fire ant mound? The same Leo who broke your heart five years ago?"

So much for playing this off as casual.

"His sister has a baby, so I think he likes kids, and I'm not asking him for any sort of commitment." Poppy felt color rise on her cheeks. "He didn't exactly break my heart. We dated a few weeks, and it didn't work out." She pointed at her cousin. "You know I was the one to break it off."

Vivienne made a noncommittal sound in her throat. "Because he flat out told you he wasn't ever going to settle down, and you're all about settling down."

"I was back then," Poppy said. "A couple of failed relationships and a broken engagement have changed me. The only commitment I'm making at the moment is to Joey. Leo wants to help, so I'm going to let him. I know he'll keep quiet because he doesn't want single women around here getting the idea that he's changed."

"What if he has changed? Maybe he has." Vivienne's eyes were bright with possibility.

Possibilities weren't something Poppy could allow herself to entertain when it came to Leo.

"I got over him a long time ago. I was engaged six months after he and I broke up."

"You know what they say about the one who got away." Vivienne did an awkward little dance move back. "Now he's back."

"Don't do this, Viv," Poppy implored. "I'm not going to lie. I appreciate the help with Joey. I know you and your mom would support me, but until the DNA comes back, it feels like it's better if I keep Joey away from the family. There are so many implications to that note that was pinned to him and…"

Vivienne held up a hand. "I get it, and the baby is

lucky to have you. Obviously, I'm here to help with anything, but I'm also kind of intrigued by the idea of Leo stepping in."

"It doesn't mean anything." Poppy wasn't going to share what Leo had said about his grandfather and his reasons for wanting to help care for Joey.

"You keep telling yourself that, but for the record, Leo made a huge mistake letting you go once."

"He isn't going to have to let me go now," Poppy insisted. "Because there isn't anything going on between us."

Vivienne shrugged. "Whatever you say, Poppy. Call or text if you need me. And give Leo a big hug for me. Or maybe a kiss. A really wet, sloppy kiss."

Poppy laughed and hugged her cousin one more time before climbing into her car. Vivienne could make all the jokes she wanted. No way would Poppy be fool enough to fall for Leo again.

After parking in her garage, she opened the door to the laundry room, wondering if she'd ever been so exhausted.

"How was the meeting?" Leo asked from where he sat cross-legged on the tile floor; two of the six-week-old kittens in her care snuggled on the towel draped across his lap while the other two attacked the plastic toy with the bell inside he flicked back and forth with one hand.

"Where's Joey?" she exclaimed as she tried to get over her shock at the scene before her. Leo did not strike her as a cat person.

"Sleeping." He nodded his head toward the monitor that sat on the dryer.

She grabbed it and studied the black-and-white screen

with disbelief. The swaddled baby slept peacefully in his crib.

"He's been down for about twenty minutes." Leo carefully moved the towel with the sleeping kittens to the cat bed and stood. "That baby likes to be held. He barely fussed as long as he was in my arms and I was moving. I might have worn a path around your first floor," he added ruefully.

"You did it," she said in wonder, more to herself than him. "You got him to sleep."

"Don't give me too much credit. I think he eventually wore himself out."

He followed her out of the laundry room. Poppy noticed the few dishes she'd left in the sink were gone, and the broom and dustpan had been put away.

"You also cleaned up and played with the kittens?" She let out a small laugh as she turned to face Leo. "You're like a mash-up of Mrs. Doubtfire and Dr. Doolittle."

His answering grin made her stomach feel like butterflies were flitting through it. "Beginner's luck," he told her with a shrug. "Tell me about the meeting."

She led the way to the family room and sat on the overstuffed leather sofa. Leo lowered himself into the matching chair on the other side of the coffee table.

"The meeting was intense, to say the least," she admitted, glancing at the monitor she held. "It's kind of difficult to believe that one sweet baby can cause so much upheaval."

"Joey didn't cause anything," Leo reminded her, and her heart pinched at his insightful words.

"True, and of course no one in my family is upset with

him. Aunt Darla wanted me to come back here and pick him up to bring him to the house. She and Vivienne are excited to meet him."

"What about your other cousins and your brothers?" Leo asked quietly as if he already knew the answer.

"Micah and Drake are as adamant as my brothers that they aren't Joey's father. All the guys, my dad and uncle Hayden included, seemed relieved that someone was watching the baby so they didn't come face-to-face with him yet. They're all on edge."

"Did you tell them that someone was me?"

"Not exactly."

Disappointment flashed in his dark gaze but was gone in an instant.

"So if none of the Fortune men are claiming him…"

She shrugged. "They all agree on DNA testing. My mom insisted it's the only way to know for sure. There are a lot of Fortunes in this state. I think she's hoping the results will confirm that no one in my family is involved."

"Makes sense." He leaned forward, placing his elbows on his knees. "Did you get the sense that any of them was hiding something?"

"I'm not much of an investigator, but they were convincing in their denials. Of course, it wouldn't be my dad. He's way too old and he and Mom are happy. I don't think Uncle Hayden would have cheated on my aunt, and Rafe is still grieving the deaths of his wife and daughter."

"That leaves Shane and your cousins…"

"I guess," she agreed with a sigh. "It would be helpful if the police had any leads on Joey's mother. I spoke with my caseworker on the drive over. She said they checked with the hospitals in the surrounding area, and there are no recorded births at any of them in the past week that could be a fit for his situation."

"Do you think he was born at home?" He frowned. "Could the cops check sales on inflatable swimming pools? Isn't that how home births work?"

Poppy made a face. "I don't honestly know, but I can't imagine any local stores are selling pools this time of year." She placed the monitor on the coffee table. "I wish there was a way I could tell Joey's mother that he's safe and being cared for. She went through the effort to leave him at my parents' house instead of…" She shook her head. "In my heart, I believe she cares about his welfare."

"There's no doubt she knows he's being cared for since she left him with your family. Despite how confusing this situation is, the Fortunes are good people." He steepled his fingers and pointed at her. "You're the best of the bunch."

Her heart leaped and butterflies flitted across her stomach at his compliment. She silently commanded herself to get a grip. The last thing needed was to let her dormant crush on Leo to rear its silly head.

"I became a foster parent to help children who needed it. It's not a big deal."

"It's a big deal, Poppy. You're a big deal."

"Your grandfather must really be having an effect," she told him before she did something pathetic like burst into tears or ask for a hug, "because you are not the same Leo Leonetti who sat across from me at dinner trying to convince both of us that he was a selfish jerk who could only prioritize himself and his work."

Harsh words, but she couldn't help it. She needed some defense against this gentle and supportive version of Leo. Otherwise, it would be too easy to put aside her commitment to guard her heart and fall for him again.

Instead of looking offended, he smiled once more. "You might be right. I want to be the kind of man Enzo would be proud to call his grandson." One thick black brow rose. "I'm not trying to rush you but seeing me help with Joey would make him happy."

He rubbed a hand along the back of his neck, and she could see the muscles in his arm bunch underneath his tailored shirt. "I'm heading to the hospital later, and it would be great to tell Papa that I'm taking his advice to heart and focusing on something besides work."

She widened her eyes at that last part.

"Someone besides myself," he added with a chuckle, "as you so eloquently pointed out."

Poppy stifled a yawn. Despite her wariness, it would be a relief to share the responsibility of caring for an infant. It might save future coffeepots from the state of the one this morning. "Okay." She swallowed back the doubts that crowded her throat.

"But this is about *Joey*," she clarified. "And if it ever gets to be too much, you need to promise to talk to me. I can't take being ghosted like…"

Of course, Leo would've heard about Michael breaking up with her. Just like he was probably well aware that her entire track record of dating was littered with relationships that hadn't worked. She didn't want him to think she'd accept his help with Joey because she hoped it would turn into something more. There wasn't room for anything more in her life at the moment, especially nothing with a man who couldn't offer her the kind of love she wanted.

"It's about Joey," he agreed. "We're friends."

"But not the kind with benefits." Poppy felt her face turn bright red but didn't lower her gaze from Leo's. His eyes darkened even more like he was imagining the two of them engaging in a mutually beneficial—

"You should go now." She stood quickly, knocking over the monitor in her haste. "I'm going to take a quick nap while Joey is asleep." She reached for the monitor but snatched back her hand when Leo's covered it. His skin was warm and soft. Tingles of awareness danced up and down her arm.

"You go nap. I'll stay for a while longer in case the baby wakes up. I've got another hour or so before they expect me at the hospital. My sisters, mom and I are taking shifts to ensure Enzo isn't alone while he's there. If it's okay with you, I'll come back around dinnertime and bring some stuff so I can stay the night. We can take turns with the whole sleep thing."

Poppy didn't know how to respond, and Leo took her stunned silence as resistance.

"I can sleep on the couch."

"We can move the crib into my office so you can have the spare bedroom," she finally said. "There's plenty of room for it in there. You'll have to use the bathroom at the end of the hall, but I have an en suite, so we won't have to share a shower."

His mouth curved just a touch on one side. "Don't worry, Poppy. But truth be told, sharing a shower with you isn't the worst fate I can imagine."

She knew he was teasing, but her body reacted just

the same. "I'm going to nap." Her voice came out sounding like a mouse on helium. She cleared her throat. "Thank you, Leo."

"Sweet dreams, Poppy."

His deep voice rumbled along her already-frayed nerve endings, and she hurried to her bedroom, wondering what in the world she'd gotten herself into.

Chapter Five

"I swear I had him on my shoulder for at least twenty minutes," Leo told his grandfather. His heart filled near to bursting as Enzo wiped tears of laughter from the corners of his eyes. "Somehow, Joey always manages to hold in his burps until he can aim his projectile spit up down the front of me."

"Babies are amazing creatures," his grandfather said with another chuckle, settling against the pillows propped behind him on the bed in his room at the family's house. "When do I get to meet little Joey? That's a nice, solid name for a lad. Short for Joseph, I assume?"

Leo shrugged. "I don't think anyone knows at this point. If you're up for a visitor, I'd love to introduce you to Poppy as well."

Enzo made a hum of approval. "I'd very much like to meet your new lady."

"Papa, we've been over this." It had been three days since he and Poppy agreed on their arrangement. As Leo had suspected, his grandfather was thrilled to hear about his involvement in caring for the abandoned baby. Joey's story had spread like wildfire through the Emerald Ridge community, although no one had come forward with any information on the little guy or his mother.

Leo couldn't be confident Enzo's rapid recovery from the setback was attributable to Leo's news. Still, the old man perked up every time he heard another story about Leo caring for the infant.

His mom and sisters also seemed shocked by his eagerness to help out and peppered him with questions about the nature of his relationship with Poppy. Leo didn't lie outright, but he didn't contradict them when they assumed there was more to it than his willingness to support an old friend.

"Poppy and I are *friends*." He shook his head and smiled at the exaggerated wink his grandfather gave him.

"Is that what the kids are calling it these days?"

"Lunch is served," his mother announced as she entered the room, holding a wooden tray with a plate of food and a glass of juice.

"Feeding me in bed like I'm an invalid," Enzo muttered, rolling his eyes. "The doctor said I'm fit as a fiddle."

"He also recommended that you take it easy for a few days." Martina never seemed to lose her patience or get flustered at how reluctant of a patient her father-in-law remained.

It reminded Leo of Poppy's unwavering patience with Joey. No matter how loudly the boy cried or how many diaper blowouts he managed, she remained gentle, nurturing and affectionate with him.

"It's warming up nicely today," Leo offered before his grandpa could argue further. "If you're feeling up to it, we could take the Polaris for a ride through the vineyards. Nothing like a bit of vitamin D to promote your healing."

"Don't you have to get back to help with the baby?" Martina asked as she placed the tray over Enzo's legs. She'd made a turkey sandwich with a caprese salad and slices of ripe apple.

"Poppy opened the spa this morning, then came home just before lunch so I could head over here," he explained. "She's going to work on promotional materials at home this afternoon while Joey naps." He held up his crossed fingers. "*Hopefully* naps."

"Where's my cookie?" Enzo asked as he dug into the sandwich.

Enzo had a legendary sweet tooth and proudly claimed that he'd enjoyed a cookie after lunch every day for the past fifty years. He'd even started baking his favorites— oatmeal raisin—after Enzo's grandmother died years earlier.

"I was thinking you might want to cut back on dessert." Martina sat at the edge of the bed.

"I have cancer. Why would I give up my cookies now?"

Leo grimaced at the matter-of-fact tone his grandfather used to describe his prognosis. They all knew it was true but hearing the future in such blunt terms made Leo's gut clench.

His mother's hands closed into fists, but she smiled. "You're right, of course. I'll bring up a cookie."

"Two," Enzo called after her. When she frowned over her shoulder, he pointed at Leo. "One for me and one for my best grandson. He's going to need all the sustenance he can get to have the energy to care for his baby."

"Not *my* baby," Leo gritted out. He suddenly felt overheated.

Martina nodded and waved a hand as she headed out of the room.

"It's difficult for her when you talk about dying," Leo told his grandfather, nipping an apple slice from the tray.

Enzo grunted. "We're all dying."

"Papa." Leo waited until his grandfather glanced up. "She worries about you. We all do."

"Okay, okay," Enzo agreed with a sigh. "I'm feeling much better now. Especially after hearing about your new lady."

Leo opened his mouth to explain to Enzo, once again, that Poppy was not *his*. But he couldn't force himself to say the words. His family understood that he was helping her as a friend—he'd been clear to make that distinction when he first told them about getting involved with Poppy and the baby. If assuming there was something more to the arrangement made his grandfather happy, who was Leo to burst that bubble?

"Poppy is amazing," he said instead, which was true. In the past few days, she'd impressed him in a myriad of ways that involved way more than simply infant care.

He'd overheard several conversations she'd had dealing with issues at the spa, and she remained calm and understanding as she offered guidance to her staff. Her brother Rafe had stopped by after dinner the previous evening.

He'd been a year younger than Leo in school, so they knew each other from playing youth sports and the close-knit Emerald Ridge social scene.

Rafe had been surprised to hear that Leo had moved into Poppy's to help with Joey. In turn, Leo hid his shock that she hadn't shared his part in caring for Joey with her family. There had been a few awkward minutes, then Poppy made a joke that eased the tension. She'd turned on the football game, and the three of them had settled in for an unexpectedly fun night of cheering on the Cowboys while Poppy and Leo took turns with Joey.

Rafe seemed vaguely interested in the baby but more curious about his sister's role as a foster parent. Poppy answered her brother's rapid-fire questions, blushing slightly when she confirmed that she was giving her romantic life a breather for now.

It wasn't fair that she had been repeatedly hurt by men and led astray by her own trusting heart. Was Leo any better than the other guys she'd dated?

Based on the mistrustful looks Rafe kept shooting him, it was evident her brother didn't think so. It was difficult to imagine the kind of loss Rafe had experienced. Leo assumed the other man's unwillingness to hold or interact with Joey had more to do with his personal history than a general dislike of babies.

Poppy didn't push her brother or make it weird. She had the innate ability to accept a person wherever they were in their life, evidenced by her willingness to allow Leo to insert himself into her orbit as if it were the most natural thing in the world. As if they were genuinely close friends, the way they pretended to be to make this arrangement seem more natural.

Even though they'd barely spoken in the past five years, Leo felt close to her. Being with Poppy and Joey made him feel part of something bigger than his work. Of course, his dedication to the winery wouldn't change, but it gave him a better understanding of why the Leonetti name and legacy were so important to his grand-father.

"Do they have any more of a clue as to the identity of the baby's mother or which Fortune is the dad?" Bella asked as she walked into the room, pulling his wandering mind back into the present moment.

"No DNA results yet," Leo told his sister.

Enzo shook his head as he finished the last bite of sandwich. "I had a friend in Italy once who had to take a paternity test. He had a reputation with the ladies but prided himself on being careful, if you know what I mean. It was the most terrifying couple days of his life until that test came back proving he wasn't a match."

"Terrifying," Bella repeated with an eye roll. "Imagine how terrified Joey's mom must have been to leave him on the Fortunes' front porch."

"You're right, of course," Enzo agreed. "I never took Garth or Hayden as the philandering type, so it must be one of those young guns."

Bella arched a delicate brow as she met Leo's gaze. "The question is which one?" she mused.

For some inexplicable reason, her pointed comment got his hackles up. He couldn't help feeling a surge of protectiveness at the thought of what this type of scandal would mean for the Fortune family and, more specifically, for Poppy.

The mystery around Joey's parents wasn't his to unravel but sharing what he knew might help quell some of the gossip around town if his sister shared the information.

"From what Poppy has told me, there's a backlog at the lab because they have so much evidence that needs to be tested with regard to the sabotage that Fortune's Gold Ranch and the other cattle operations in the area are experiencing."

Bella whistled under her breath as she stepped forward to lift the tray off the bed. "This is more drama than Emerald Ridge has seen in years."

"Why would someone want to damage the cattle ranches?" Enzo threw his hands in the air. "Those families are an integral part of this community."

"Maybe it's someone outside the community," she suggested. "It could be hired thugs from a different area of the state who want to hurt the success of the ranches around here. Particularly FGR, since they're the biggest and most profitable."

"You're watching too much true-crime TV," Leo told his sister, hoping her supposition wasn't true. "Likely they're going to find out it's high school kids carrying out pranks that have gone too far."

"Don't be naive," Bella said, her tone sharp. "Whoever is behind the sabotage could come after our vineyard next. What if someone has general beef with the town and everyone in it?"

"Beef. Cattle ranches." Enzo chuckled. "I see what you did there."

"I'm serious, Papa. Leo needs to take a potential threat seriously, too. As *CEO*—" she placed a particular emphasis on that word "—you need to look out for the vineyard's safety. Maybe hire an outside firm to watch the vines at night?"

It was a bone of contention when Leo had been named the head of the company after their father's death. Bella had always been the most interested in the vineyard.

Since Leo was the eldest of his siblings, it made sense as far as a line of succession, but he knew his sister believed his getting the title—which he hadn't necessarily wanted—had more to do with his gender than birth order.

She'd become an expert on the grapes, and he'd named her head vintner for the operation when his late father's right-hand man retired. At this point, they all worked in concert, each with autonomy in their specific area of expertise—Leo as the head of the company, Bella overseeing the winemaking, Antonia in charge of finances, and the extroverted baby of the family, Gia, handling the marketing and PR. Sometimes, however, the past grievance popped up like a headstrong weed in a garden.

"I'll look into it," he promised. If Bella thought extra security measures were important, he took it seriously.

"So what about the Fortunes and their DNA?" Placated, she turned the topic back to one Leo did not want to discuss.

"Like I said, the lab is backed up. Only two results have come back so far. Shane and Rafe are not Joey's father."

Both his grandfather and sister seemed to consider that.

"Two down, four to go." Bella picked up the tray from the dresser. "I need to head over to the barrel room and check on the fermentation. If you bring Papa around for a drive, stop by." She smiled at the old man. "I have a new blend I want you to sample."

"Can't wait." Enzo beamed at his granddaughter, who'd inherited her love of tending the vines from him.

She left the room and Enzo turned his gaze to Leo.

"I might take a short nap before we head out." The old man gave a wide yawn.

"If it's too much for you—"

"A nap will refresh me," Enzo interrupted. "Come back in an hour. It's been too long since I've felt the energy of the vines. It will do me good." He reached out and clasped Leo's hand. "Just like hearing stories of your new domestic adventure does. Plan a time to bring Poppy and the baby to see me, Leo. I don't want to miss a thing."

"You won't," he promised even as his heart ached knowing it was a vow he couldn't keep forever. His grandfather sank back again. His eyes drifted shut, and Leo silently walked out of the room. He owed Poppy Fortune big-time for fostering this new opportunity to connect with his grandfather.

Without overthinking it, he pulled his phone from the back pocket of his jeans and sent a quick text checking in on her day. She responded within seconds with a selfie of her smiling at the camera while holding Leo in her arms. Humphrey's fluffy head rested on her shoulder.

He *liked* the photograph and smiled as he headed out of the back of the house and toward the winery's main office. There were several ongoing initiatives he needed to check on. Typically, he had no problem working through lunch, dinner and late into the night. But now he had the urge to finish as quickly as possible and get back to Poppy and Joey. Oddly, he missed them even though he'd only been away for a few hours.

At the sound of the doorbell, Humphrey let out a barrage of excited woofs, and Poppy jumped up from the sofa where she was working on her laptop. She shushed the dog as she rushed toward the front door. Joey had been asleep for only ten minutes after another afternoon of on-and-off crying, so Poppy sent up a silent prayer the dog wouldn't wake him.

Annoyance flickered through her as she opened the door, already admonishing Leo. "You can come in. I told you that you didn't have to knock, especially—"

She paused midsentence as Courtney Wellington gave her a dubious look, the late-afternoon sky dusky purple behind her. "It's not smart for a single lady to allow unannounced guests to simply walk into your house." However, the woman seemed to have no problem striding past without being invited.

"That's not what this is." Poppy slowly closed the door behind her. "I was expecting someone else."

Courtney's eyes gleamed. "And who would that be?"

Poppy fidgeted and tried to come up with an answer that would be evasive but not an outright lie. She wasn't trying to keep the fact that Leo was staying with her a secret. Yet she didn't feel like advertising it either, especially to Courtney, who could make something sordid out of even the most innocent arrangement.

Even though Poppy's family knew about Leo, none of them seemed inclined to question her decision. They were consumed with both the rash of vandalism being committed against local ranches and the mystery surrounding the abandoned baby, so no one had time to worry about her situation. She hoped the same could be said for Courtney, although that seemed like a stretch.

"What can I do for you?" Poppy gestured toward the laptop and stack of papers on the coffee table. "I'm trying to get through some work while Joey's napping, so this isn't the best time for a visit."

"I brought you a baby gift," Courtney said with a sniff. Poppy immediately felt guilty for her rudeness. "It's a blanket with his name embroidered on it." She handed over the shopping bag. "It will help him always know who he is."

Poppy pulled out a fleece blanket with an appliquéd illustration of a horse and the name Joey Fortune embroidered below it in a bold font.

"He's going to be first of the next generation in line to inherit FGR," Courtney pointed out. "Although I suppose depending on which generation of men is responsible, he could be your new baby brother."

Poppy refolded the blanket and tried not to grit her teeth too obviously. "My father is not Joey's father," she said, unsure why she felt so certain about it but unwilling to show any doubt in front of the other woman, who tsked in response.

"I suppose that remains to be seen. I texted your mother to see if more DNA results had come back. I didn't get a response from her. She must be beside herself and the implications this scandal could have for her family's good name."

"Why do you sound happy about that?"

Courtney blinked her heavily shadowed eyes. "Isn't that a cheeky thing to say? I want to support your mother and aunt. You as well, if you need me."

"I don't," Poppy said without missing a beat. "Thank you for the gift, Courtney, but I have plenty of support so—"

At that moment, the front door opened, and Leo walked

in. While Poppy was relieved to see him, she was not thrilled at the shocked gasp Courtney let out.

"*This* is who you were expecting?" Courtney rolled her lips together as if trying to hold back a comment. Poppy could imagine what the woman would say to her: What was she thinking to let a man like Leo back into her life?

She could deny it all she wanted, but he had the power to hurt her. Yes, they were becoming friends and she appreciated his help but none of that changed the fact that she'd have to work hard to keep her heart out of the mix where Leo was concerned.

"Hello, Mrs. Wellington," he said as he walked toward them.

"Oh, honey, please call me Courtney. Mrs. Wellington makes me feel ancient."

There was a predatory glint in Courtney's eyes as she gave Leo a thorough once-over. Poppy had the urge to step in front of him like a shield, although he didn't need her protection. He was an experienced man. Maybe he was into older women. At the realization that his love life was none of her business, Poppy's mouth felt coated in sawdust.

"Leo and I are old friends," she said, sounding prim even to her own ears. "He's helping me with Joey since the placement was so sudden."

Courtney didn't take her eyes off Leo. "I'm sure he could help you with any number of things…"

Leo visibly blanched. "I think I hear Joey fussing. I'll go check on him."

"I don't hear anything," Courtney cooed. "I've been

meaning to pay a visit to your winery, Leo. Perhaps we could arrange a private tour."

"My sister Gia handles the tours, and I'm sure she can set something up. I really need to check on Joey." As if on cue, the video monitor crackled, and they heard the sound of a baby's cry.

Leo looked visibly relieved. "Nice to see you, Mrs. Welling— Nice to see you again, Courtney."

Poppy almost laughed at the speed with which Leo hightailed it out of the family room.

She turned back to Courtney. "I should probably get dinner started."

If the woman hadn't been Botoxed within an inch of her life, her eyebrows likely would have hit the top of her forehead. Instead, she conveyed her shock with a gaping open mouth. "Are you shacking up with Leo Leonetti?" she asked.

Poppy pressed her lips together. "Such a crude phrase, but no. As I said, Leo is a friend, and he's helping with Joey."

"And whatever other kind of late-night assistance you might need." Courtney winked, and it was a wonder her eyelashes didn't stick together.

"Bottle-feeding and diaper changes," Poppy muttered. She didn't owe their nosy neighbor an explanation but felt compelled to clarify again that nothing was happening between her and Leo. It was a good reminder for herself as well.

"Thanks again for stopping by," she said, moving to the front door. "I'll let my mom know you were asking after her."

Courtney glanced at the baby monitor. Leo was singing an old Johnny Cash song as he danced around the room with Joey in his arms. "That's unexpected." She sounded awestruck.

Poppy quickly scooped up the monitor, turned it off and then placed her hand on Courtney's lower back to give her a gentle push toward the door.

"Whatever it takes to soothe a baby," Poppy said cheerily.

Courtney allowed herself to be shown out the door but turned back and gripped Poppy's wrist. "Watch out for that one, girl. He's got a reputation that a woman like you might not want to invite into her life." She paused, then added in a low whisper, "Into her *bed*."

Poppy's face flamed, but she kept her features neutral. "Bottle-feedings and diaper changes," she repeated. "Have a good night, Courtney."

Leo appeared with Joey in his arms just as she turned from the closed door.

"Is it weird to say I feel violated?" He gave a mock shudder. "I've heard stories about Mr. Wellington's widow, but this is the first time I've had that close an interaction with her. Next time, I'm renting a shark cage."

She shook her head but smiled. "For your sake, I hope there won't be a next time. How's our best boy?"

"Pretty sure he's hungry. I'll make a bottle."

"That would be great," Poppy said, grateful for Leo's constant willingness to pitch in. She wasn't sure what she'd do without him. Obviously, she shouldn't get used to it. After all, she'd known what she was getting into as a single foster parent but hadn't expected her first placement to be an infant.

Having Leo around made everything easier, and she

doubted he even realized what a huge impact he was having on her. Despite what had happened between them in the past, it was easy to believe this arrangement could develop into something more—that the three of them might make a real family.

But was she just setting herself up for more heartbreak?

"Everything okay?"

She blinked to find Leo staring at her from the edge of the open-concept kitchen.

"What? I mean, yes." She gave him a quick thumbs-up. "Just a bit tired."

"I can take overnight duty," Leo offered as he balanced Joey in one arm and measured scoops of powdered formula with his free hand.

"It's fine," she assured him. "I'm fine. I'll start dinner."

"About that…" Leo glanced over his shoulder at her, and Poppy's stomach did that annoying pitch and tingle again. "My mom made us a lasagna. I forgot to bring it in, so it's still in the back seat of my car."

"You feed babies, take overnight shifts and provide dinner." She forced out a laugh. "Better not let this get out, Leo Leonetti, or there will be no level of commitment phobia that will keep the women around here from descending on you."

She expected him to crack a joke in response, but his gaze was serious as he turned to face her fully. "But you'll protect me, Poppy. You'll keep me safe, right?"

In a way, that was its own kind of joke, but she also felt something shift deep in her heart. Leo didn't need her protection—not with Courtney or any other woman— except what if he did? What if this man, who was so guarded and yet possessed a generous heart, needed to feel safe and cared for just for being him?

Poppy couldn't offer him much in return for his help with Joey, but she could give him refuge from whatever feelings and worries weighed on him.

"I've got you, Leo," she said softly.

His eyes flared like he hadn't expected her to take his request seriously. The air between them changed in that moment. It grew heavy and charged. She could practically see sparks flickering between them.

Joey squirmed and whimpered, and the invisible tether that connected them broke apart. "I'll grab the lasagna," she offered, turning for the door.

"Thanks," Leo called but she didn't answer.

Poppy hurried down the porch steps, then stopped and looked up at the stars blanketing the February night sky. She needed to be reminded that there was a big universe beyond the cozy walls of her house. Her attraction to Leo—her emotions—were tiny in comparison. Tiny and insignificant, even if it didn't feel that way in her heart.

Chapter Six

Leo walked into Coffee Connection, the popular coffee shop and bakery in downtown Emerald Ridge later that week. He paused as he noticed all three of his sisters sitting at the table in front of the window waiting for him. Gia had invited him to meet, and she guiltily dropped her gaze when he glared. He had half a mind to turn on his heel and walk back out. He loved his sisters, but this was clearly an ambush.

"Don't even think about it," Bella, the oldest of the sisters, commanded, pointing a finger at him. She'd always been the bossiest of the trio.

"We ordered you a chocolate chip scone," Gia told him. "Your favorite." Her smile was coaxing, which, despite his affection for her, didn't give him the slightest bit of encouragement.

"And a double-shot espresso," Antonia added. "We figured you could use all the caffeine you can get right now."

It must be serious if the three of them were being so accommodating—two out of the three, anyway. Things would be end-of-the-world dire if Bella ever became accommodating.

Yet even with his disrupted sleep schedule, Leo felt

more energized than he had in a long time. He also knew little Joey wasn't entirely to blame for his wonky sleep patterns. He and Poppy took turns keeping the baby's monitor overnight, but even when she was responsible for late-night feedings and diaper changes, Leo seemed to be attuned to Joey's cycles.

Not to mention the dreams he had on a regular basis starring Poppy—the not-in-any-way-platonic dreams that woke him. Seeing her selfless heart on display with Joey made her even more alluring than she'd been when during that short time they'd dated. Last night, he'd blinked awake just in time to hear her opening the door to the baby's bedroom. He knew she'd be wearing one of the sets of quirky pajama pants and T-shirts from her collection of cartoon characters and animal prints.

Leo had never considered himself a connoisseur of women's sleepwear. He was typically too preoccupied with taking it off to pay much attention to lacy camisoles or complicated lingerie with straps and clasps. Getting worked up over shapeless cat-print pajamas that showed nothing of Poppy's trim curves bordered on pathetic. He cleared his throat as he slid into the chair across from Gia.

"Are you getting sick?" Antonia asked. "Your face is flushed."

Bella, who occupied the chair beside him, reached over and placed her cool hand on his forehead. "I don't think he's feverish."

Gia was already pushing back from the table. "I'll order you a cup of their medicinal tea blend. It'll wipe out any cold or flu nasties you have coming on."

"I'm not sick," Leo muttered. He couldn't exactly

share with his sisters what had prompted the color to rise to his cheeks. "I don't need to be coddled by the three of you. Save it for Papa."

"He's not a cooperative patient either." Bella reached over and broke off the corner of his scone.

"Hey, that's the best part."

"I know." She elbowed him gently. "It's why I took it."

Leo couldn't help but smile. Bella had been nipping bites off his plate since they were kids. "So what is the purpose behind this unexpected tribunal?"

He lifted the cup to his lips and took a moment to savor the nutty richness of the dark liquid, although it didn't offer the same pleasure he usually derived from the shop's famous coffee.

Poppy's maker had a built-in timer, and since she'd replaced the broken pot, he awoke most mornings to the smell of freshly ground beans brewing in the kitchen. It was a vast improvement over the swill he typically made for himself.

No one in his family understood how Leo had never learned to make a decent cup of coffee. His father had prided himself on the espressos he turned out from the fancy Italian machine in Leo's parents' kitchen. One of Leo's most vivid memories as a kid was coming out of his room on weekends—he'd never been a late sleeper—and going to sit quietly with his father at the kitchen table.

Franco would sip his morning espresso while Leo poured orange juice into a matching cup. He knew better than to talk to his father before he finished that first cup, but he still missed those moments of companionable silence.

Growing up with three sisters, there was very little quiet, and he'd welcomed the day he finally moved out and into his own place, even if it was only a quarter mile from his childhood home. He enjoyed the solitude of coming home to a silent house. Yet when he'd stopped by this morning to pick up some items he wanted to bring to Poppy's, the stillness of the empty house struck him as sad. After a few days at Poppy's with her sunny presence, plus the noise from the dog and menagerie of cats, not to mention Joey's cries, his house seemed cold and uninviting.

He hated to admit that he didn't look forward to returning to it after Joey was placed in a permanent home, but a part of him couldn't deny it.

"We want to talk about you and Poppy Fortune," Antonia said after a moment.

Leo blinked. "What about us?" he forced himself to ask. Honestly, he didn't want to know what his siblings would have to say on the subject.

"Gia stopped by the spa yesterday," Bella explained.

Gia nodded. "I talked to Poppy."

"She works there." Leo frowned. "Did you come over to FGR to check up on me?"

His youngest sister rolled her yes. "Of course not. I wanted to book a Galentine's Day treatment for the three of us and Mom. We thought we'd treat her to—"

"What is *Galentine's* Day?"

"Get with the program, bro." Bella nabbed another bite of scone. "It's a holiday that celebrates female friendships."

"The day before Valentine's Day," Gia clarified, then

leaned across the table. "You do remember that next week is Valentine's Day?"

He tried not to fidget under her scrutiny. "February 14. I know the date. But I'm not dating anyone."

"You're *living* with a woman," Antonia said.

"We're friends," he muttered.

"That's what Poppy told me, too." Gia shook her head. "It doesn't make sense."

"You aren't some kind of generous, always-do-the-right-thing type of guy," Bella told him.

Leo rubbed two fingers against his chest. "Ouch."

"No offense." Bella lifted her palms in the air. "You're great, bro, but we figured you spouted out the line about being friends to protect your privacy. Rude, by the way, when we're your family. We don't have secrets. So there must be something more to it. It's a big thing you're doing, Leo."

"Maybe I'm a better man than you three give me credit for." He crossed his arms over his chest, irritation pulsing through him even though his sisters were right.

Antonia made a tsking sound that reminded Leo of their mother. "You're not romantically involved with Poppy?"

"She's got a lot on her plate right now," he said.

"Which is a nonanswer," his middle sister pointed out.

"Poppy and I tried dating a few years ago. We weren't a match."

Bella scoffed. "Back then, you weren't the type of guy who would have offered to help her raise an abandoned child."

"We do think you're a great guy," Gia said with a

smile. "And we like Poppy a lot. She said the nicest things about you."

He clamped his jaw shut so he wouldn't ask *what things*. "She wants something different than I can give her. She deserves someone who can provide that."

His sisters exchanged looks among themselves.

"Don't do that silent-female-conversation thing right in front of me," he complained.

Gia smiled. "Poppy looked smitten when she talked about you."

"I'm helping her out with Joey. She's grateful."

"She *likes* you," Antonia said. "Not just because you change diapers."

"Although a man willing to change diapers is hot," Bella said with a laugh. "Do you load and unload the dishwasher, too?"

"Um…sure…if it needs it."

"Also hot."

"Loading dishes is not hot," Leo argued. "I haven't even taken Poppy out on a date since we've reconnected."

"Maybe you should change that," Antonia suggested.

"We'll babysit," Gia offered. "Mom would be over the moon. Papa, too, to have a baby around again. Especially one that's yours."

"You're the favorite," Bella grumbled but there was a smile in her voice.

"Joey isn't mine." Leo forced himself to say the words even though the statement made his chest ache. "Poppy either."

"But she could be," Gia countered. "If you aren't a dum-dum."

"Dum-dum. Is that a technical term?" Leo shot back.

"She likes you," Antonia said again. "We think you like her, too."

"A lot," Bella added.

Leo glared at her. "You don't know that."

His opinionated eldest sister nodded, confirming the opinions of the other two like she was their queen. "We know."

He felt his face go hot again like he did have a fever. If only this *were* a fever dream and one he could wake up from quickly. "I don't do commitment," he argued. "Everyone knows that. Poppy knows that."

Gia shrugged. "You haven't until now, but things change."

"Nothing has changed," he practically shouted then counted to ten in his head when several customers at the tables nearby looked his way. Everything had changed, but he wasn't willing to admit it, not even to himself. He'd only been staying with Poppy a week, but their routine felt natural in a way he hadn't expected.

Nothing would come of it. He had too much to handle running the winery, wrangling his sisters and helping his mom take care of Enzo. A relationship was out of the question, and Joey was temporary. What would he and Poppy have without the baby to bind them together?

A chance at a future together, an annoying voice inside his heart whispered. He shook his head to loosen the grip of those fanciful thoughts. Even if he gave them a chance, he'd likely mess it up. Again. He couldn't risk it. He *wouldn't* risk the kind of pain that would cause them both.

"I asked Poppy to let me help," he told his sisters. "Not because I'm kind or generous or anywhere near the unselfish person she is. Papa and I had a heated conversation the night before his oxygen levels dropped."

Leo kept his gaze on the crumbs scattered across the empty plate. He couldn't watch his sisters' faces go from hopeful to disappointed. "He was nagging me to settle down or at least put more emphasis on having a life outside of work."

"Not terrible advice," Gia said quietly.

"There's nothing wrong with being dedicated to work," Bella countered.

"I don't want to upset him again," Leo continued, wrapping one hand around the now-cooled coffee mug. "He's been in such good spirits lately, but things went sideways when we had dinner. The next morning, he'd had the setback." He swallowed around the lump in this throat. "Then I saw Poppy in the hospital cafeteria, and she told me about Joey. She's the best person I know, exactly the kind of woman Papa would want for me. I asked her—*begged* practically—if I could help with the baby because it would make him happy."

Silence met his revelation, and he finally glanced up. "It worked. He loves hearing my stories about taking care of Joey."

Gia smiled, but it looked forced. "You're lying to him."

"You're lying to all of us," Antonia added. "Are you and Poppy even friends?"

"We are now." Leo tried not to flinch under his middle sister's scrutiny. "I really like her, and I think she likes me." He shrugged. "I'm pretty likable, you know."

"Oh, Leo." Bella's sigh was one for the ages. "The

truth is you're lying to yourself most of all. It doesn't matter how this arrangement came to be."

"It doesn't?" Antonia demanded.

"What matters," Gia continued, "is what you're going to do now. You like her. She likes you. Don't mess it up."

"I'm not," he protested, hands up. "I won't."

None of the women looked convinced.

"There's nothing to mess up. We aren't together." Leo wasn't sure why he insisted on arguing for a fact that made his gut twist. Poppy might not have had the best luck with men, but that was bound to change. She was too fantastic to remain alone forever. She had so much love to give and whatever man was on the receiving end of it would be lucky indeed.

Why couldn't it be him? At least temporarily.

"It's a good thing we're here to knock some sense into you." Gia reached across the table and rapped her knuckles on his forehead. "You're living with her. You're taking care of a baby with her. You are together in all the ways that count."

"Not *all* the ways," Bella said with a laugh.

"You can change that, Leo," Antonia advised him. "Bella's right. Do more than not mess it up. Step up and make something more happen. Poppy deserves a man who makes her feel special."

"She *is* special."

"Then it shouldn't be hard," Bella said.

Right. It would be easy to take his relationship with Poppy to a new level. Hell, sometimes it felt like he wanted to kiss her more than he wanted his next breath.

"What if she says no?"

"You've got charm for days," Gia told him. "Put it to good use."

He nodded and pushed back from the table. "Charming. I can do that. Thanks for the coffee and scone." He grinned at the three of them. "And the advice."

"We give great advice," Gia confirmed.

"Because we love you," Antonia added.

Bella smirked. "Also, we don't want you to be a dum-dum."

"I think I can handle that," he promised. Could he handle it? He'd certainly try his best. How hard could it be when he already cared for Poppy? Wanted to kiss her. Nope, no kissing. Not unless they could agree to new terms involving no-strings-attached benefits. She might be willing. If he was able to convince her it would be fun for them both. It would be his great pleasure to make it fun for her.

Time to turn on the patented Leonetti charm.

"Do you have something in your eye?" Poppy asked Leo as they stood at the bend on the nature trail. "Want me to take a look?"

He went absolutely still as he stared at her. "I'm winking at you."

"Oh." She glanced down at the top of Joey's round head covered by another soft cap. The baby was fast asleep, lulled by the rhythmic motion of the two-mile hike Leo had suggested they take Saturday morning.

Poppy had been surprised at first. She assumed Leo would use the weekend as an excuse to get some space from her and Joey. Not that he ever acted like staying with her was cramping his style. But it had to be, right?

Based on how the women talked at the spa, Leo was one of Emerald Ridge's most eligible and elusive bachelors. Poppy knew this from personal experience and also understood the motivation behind why he'd offered to help with Joey. Neither changed the fact that his dedication and care felt real. He seemed as happy to be a part of her life as she was to have him there.

She figured that was a part of the deal. Leo's commitment to a goal he set for himself left no room for doubt. The growth and success of Leonetti Vineyards under his leadership proved that. Spending a quiet Saturday with Joey and her felt like extra credit. And the winking...

"*Why* are you winking?"

"Because it's charming?" He laughed, sounding embarrassed at being called out. "I was trying to flirt with you, Poppy."

"Oh." She repeated the word on an exhalation. Her mind reeled as she tried to come up with a reason *why* he'd be flirting with her. That went above and beyond the parameters of their arrangement.

"I guess my skills in the charm department are a little rusty." He seemed as befuddled as she felt.

She shifted as an abrupt breeze blew up from the nearby creek, barely a trickle of water at this time of year. She shielded Joey from the gust. "I'm sure your skills are as sharp as ever, Leo. It's me. I didn't expect to be on the receiving end of your..." She shook her head. "Of any of this."

He stepped closer and, whether on purpose or instinctual, shifted his body so that he sheltered *her* from the wind. It had been a long time since someone—a man in particular—had acted the least bit protective of Poppy.

She had a type, and it was men who let her do the care-giving as if she should feel privileged to dote on them and cater to their needs.

Leo's intuitive ability to make her feel special in little ways was a much more powerful aphrodisiac than all the winking in the world.

"Why not?" he asked, genuinely curious. "I like you, Poppy. I always have."

He reached out and tucked a stray lock of hair behind her ear, his finger skimming her sensitive skin. Goose bumps erupted, and she had trouble remembering to breathe.

"I like you, too." Her voice was husky, and she should have been embarrassed, but Leo's mouth crooked into a grin.

"I'm going to kiss you now." He spoke softly as if he didn't want to startle her. "If that's okay with you?"

No, no, no. She'd told herself she was taking a break from romantic entanglements, and her heart was already half lost to Leo and his unexpected thoughtfulness. The only thing keeping her safe was knowing their arrangement included only friendship. A kiss would change everything.

"Yes," she said, ignoring all the warning bells clanging in her brain. Because more than being safe, at the moment, she wanted Leo's mouth on hers.

She knew how it felt to kiss Leo. They may have gone on only a few dates two years ago, but they also shared several passionate kisses. Those kisses had muddled her resolve when it came time to end things after he told her he had no interest in the future she wanted.

Now he pressed his lips to hers with a tenderness she

didn't expect. He cupped her cheeks with his hands and wasn't she a sucker for that gesture?

Leo's kiss felt brand-new, a reintroduction of sorts. Like he wanted to know her in a different way than he had before. But he already knew how to make her feel wanted. It simply wasn't enough. He could be holding back out of respect for her or a healthy dose of caution, but she wanted to forget about smart and throw caution to the wind.

Poppy wasn't inexperienced, but she'd never been assertive. This felt like a new version of her—one she wanted to discover with Leo. She traced her tongue across the seam of his lips, and he let out a barely audible groan as he opened for her.

A wave of lust-filled power rushed through her. She went along for the ride without thinking about the crash that might come on the other side. He moved in closer, as close as he could get with a baby between them. Poppy lost herself in the feel of Leo's warmth, his strength and the heady intoxication of knowing that he was just as affected as her.

He seemed content to savor their kisses without pushing for more, not that anything more could occur in this setting.

When Joey fidgeted and let out a tiny cry, Poppy would have jumped away like she'd been caught making out in the basement by her father. Instead, Leo lowered his hands to her shoulders and eased her back slowly.

"I like you." His eyes were dark with passion. "I like kissing you. I'd like more, but only if you want it."

Poppy wanted more…more than was prudent for either of them. The type that could put her guarded heart at risk if she wasn't careful. She opened her mouth to answer, but he placed a finger against her lips, then bent down and dropped a gentle kiss on Joey's head. He adjusted the hat the boy wore to cover his ears more fully.

"Don't answer now," Leo told her gruffly. "I want you to think about it. I want you to be certain. I'm not going anywhere, Poppy, so you'll know where to find me. For as long as you need me." The words sounded like a promise, then he pointed to the western sky. "But we should head back before those clouds get any closer."

"Right." Poppy nodded and started down the trail toward the parking lot. It was good that he'd told her not to answer. She needed time to figure out how much she could give Leo without losing herself in the process.

Chapter Seven

Poppy unstrapped Joey from his infant seat, picked him up and walked toward the main barn of the FGR guest ranch later that afternoon.

Although Leo had planned to spend the entire day with her after the hike, he'd gotten called to the winery to deal with a personnel issue that couldn't wait. He promised to return before dinner, but she felt restless in the house without him.

Perhaps her inability to settle had more to do with the nerves tingling along her spine every time she thought about the kiss she and Leo had shared and his comment about wanting more.

Now that the moment had passed, she should file it away as a fantastic but one-and-done situation. Getting more involved romantically—or at least intimately—with Leo could only end in disaster.

She couldn't seem to convince her heart or body. She'd always been one for commitment and knew full well Leo wasn't interested in the same thing. But that had gotten her nowhere. It might be time to try something different.

Her feelings for him didn't necessarily change her opinion about relationships. It was much easier to concentrate on work and Joey than think about trying to find love again. So if she wasn't worried about falling in love or having her heart broken, being with Leo wouldn't be as big of a deal as she feared.

She'd been unable to stand pacing back and forth in the house. Going to her parents' didn't seem like a decent option, as seeing Joey was still difficult for her mother. There'd been a delay in getting some of the DNA results returned, and the tension within the family kept ramping up.

So Poppy headed for her second-favorite place on the ranch after her beloved spa, the FGR horse barn.

While the temperature had reached the midfifties today, Joey was bundled up in a hooded one-piece in a dusty periwinkle color. She hadn't wanted to take a chance on him catching a chill in the sometimes-drafty barn. Maybe an experienced mother wouldn't worry about that, but she preferred to err on the side of caution where the baby was concerned.

Although she was well aware her time as his foster mother could end at any point, it hadn't stopped her from falling deeply in love with him. There were so many things about the baby that were easy to adore…

The way he smiled and the tiny gurgling noises he made after a feeding was just one example. How his little legs kicked during diaper changes like he was happy to have them free. And he seemed so content when she or Leo bathed him, glad to stay in the warm water until the skin on his little fingers turned pruny. She had a feeling Joey would grow into a kid who loved summers and swimming. It hurt her heart, knowing she would likely not witness that joy.

Unless, of course, her cousin Micah turned out to be his father. That was the DNA test that had yet to come back, along with her father and uncle Hayden. She couldn't even consider that either of the older men might be Joey's father.

She forced herself to draw in a deep breath and then exhaled her worries about the identity of Joey's mother and father—for the moment, anyway. She'd come to the barn to clear her head, and that's what she intended to do.

The horses she wanted to visit were standing in a group in the pasture behind the reclaimed wood structure, so she walked to the fence line. Balancing the baby in one arm, she pulled a handful of cut carrots out of her jacket pocket. She kissed the air, and immediately Pecan, a chestnut mare and one of Poppy's personal favorites of the trail horses at the ranch, ambled over to her.

"Hey, sweetheart," she cooed, holding out her open palm. The large horse whinnied and gently took the carrots from her hand with a snuffle.

The noise startled Joey, who scrunched up his face as if he might let out a wail, but when Pecan leaned over to sniff his belly with her soft nose, he immediately calmed. One of his hands shot up as if to pet the big animal.

Tears sprang to Poppy's eyes as she witnessed the sweet interaction between the baby and the horse. There were so many moments and milestones she wanted to share with Joey. In her secret heart of hearts, she wondered what would happen if they couldn't locate his mother, and the DNA tests proved that no one in her family had fathered him. He could still be a Fortune, just like the note said. He could be *hers*. *Poppy's*.

"You're such a good girl," she told Pecan, her voice trembling.

She'd been warned about getting too close to any child assigned to her but wasn't sure how to help it. Could she talk to Leo about all this, or would that scare him away?

"Hey, Pop-Tart."

She glanced over her shoulder, keeping one hand on Pecan's head, to see Shane ambling toward her from the ranch's business office. It overlooked this part of the paddock so she imagined he'd seen her through his office window. Her brothers had a million nicknames for her. Pop-Tart. Popsicle. Popcorn. As a kid, it had annoyed her to no end, but now she smiled at the silly term of endearment.

"To what do I owe the pleasure of this visit? Are you looking to go for a ride? I could saddle up—"

He broke off as Poppy turned to him fully, and his gaze settled on Joey.

Other than the women in her family and Rafe when he'd briefly stopped over, no one else had met the baby.

"I needed to get out of the house. It's such a nice day… I thought I'd bring him to meet some of the horses. It's never too early for a Fortune to be introduced to life on the ranch, right?"

Shane ran a hand through his dark hair and seemed to consider her question even though she'd posed it rhetorically.

"Do you really think one of us is his father?"

"If I'm being honest, I hope none of you is Joey's father."

Shane nodded. "I get it. Brady is a bundle of energy

at six, but it's fun energy. It's a lot tougher when they're babies, and I imagine the foster parent gig is a tough one and probably already getting to be a drag. If he's not part of our family then…"

"It's not that." Poppy couldn't believe her brother would suggest such a thing and swatted him on the arm. She knew how much he loved his son and maintained a cordial relationship with his ex-wife for Brady's benefit. "I hope none of you is the father because I can't imagine somebody in our family treating a woman so poorly that she would resort to leaving her baby on someone's front porch step."

"Of course." Shane cringed. "I spoke without thinking." Pecan snorted as if she couldn't believe the comment either. She shook her head then moseyed back toward the other horses since snack time was over.

"Maybe you should have a big glass of water to wash down the foot lodged firmly in your mouth." Poppy continued to glare at her brother. "I love Joey already. I would love for him to be part of this family—for him to be part of *my* family. I just…"

Shane's jaw went slack, and she realized she'd just given voice to her most secret wish, the one she couldn't share with anyone. So much for keeping her emotions to herself since she'd blurted them right out. "I know being a foster parent is a temporary arrangement." She licked her dry lips.

"Not always, Pop Rocks. If they can't track down the mom or figure out who the father is through DNA testing, this baby is going to need a permanent home." He offered a tentative smile. "You would be an excellent mother."

"I'm on my own," she whispered because along with her deepest desire came her deepest fear. "They might think I'm unfit to adopt a baby because I don't have a partner."

Shane gripped the fence post as he looked out over the pasture. Other than Brady, he spent more time with the herd of ranch horses than people most weeks, and he seemed to like it that way.

To her surprise, he reached forward and lifted Joey from her arms. "You aren't alone. Not that you couldn't handle raising a child if you were, but no matter what those DNA test results show, if you want this baby to be a Fortune, we've got your back. Plus, Brady would be over the moon."

She leaned in and hugged her brother. He was tall like Rafe, both of them over six feet, and she took comfort in his strength and the words that reminded her how lucky she was to be a part of this family.

"He's a cute kid." Shane ruffled her hair as she pulled back from the hug. "Although I wouldn't say he looks like any of us."

"He's not even a month old." Poppy smoothed a finger over Joey's soft cheek. The baby was wide-eyed, like he wanted to check out everything around him. "Leo says he looks like a grumpy old man, especially when his face scrunches up to make a poo."

Shane barked out a laugh. "I never thought I'd hear the day when Leo Leonetti was making jokes about baby poo."

"He's been a huge help," Poppy said, that annoying protectiveness where Leo was concerned rising to the surface again.

Her brother seemed to consider that as he lifted his head to take in the open fields again. "I like the guy. It's just a surprise that he's stepped in to be there for you and the baby in this way."

"I don't know what I'd do without him."

Shane's gaze met hers. "Because of Joey or because you're falling for him?"

It was a good thing Poppy wasn't a gambler since she seemed to have no poker face. Still, she offered a bland smile. "We're friends." The words threatened to stick in her throat, but she forced them out. "When Joey no longer needs me, Leo and I will return to our regularly scheduled lives."

Her brother didn't look like he believed her. One of the ranch hands stepped out of the barn and called Shane's name. "I've got to get back to work." He deposited Joey back into her arms. "You're doing a good thing, Pop. Just remember you aren't doing it alone."

Poppy nodded, tears stinging the backs of her eyes. It felt like her heart had opened in a different way since Joey entered her life. All of her resolve to guard it could be struck down with a kind word or one of the baby's sweet smiles.

Not ready to return home, she walked into the barn, pointing out the equipment and tack to the baby like he could understand her. Her mind wandered to Leo and the heated kiss they'd shared. Did she truly want more? Could she handle it?

Yes, her body whispered. *A thousand times yes*.

She knew better than to let desire lead. Or love for that matter. A broken engagement had at least taught her that.

But she also wasn't naive and believed what she'd told her brother. This arrangement with Leo was temporary, and she simply needed to keep her feelings that way, too.

It was nearly ten, the night sky dotted with sparkling stars, before Leo let himself into Poppy's house. The personnel issue had taken far too long to handle, and then his grandfather insisted he stay for dinner and a few rounds of cards with him and Leo's mother.

He understood that the old man, claiming to feel totally back to normal, was chafing under the doctor's orders to continue taking it easy for a few weeks. Thin lines of tension bracketed Martina's mouth as she worked to keep her father-in-law compliant with his schedule of rest-and-modified-activity.

Leo had texted Poppy to explain, and of course, she hadn't pushed back. She never seemed to demand more of him than he was willing to freely give.

But it rankled him that their romantic interlude had been cut short, and their kiss now felt like a whole world away instead of something that had occurred a few hours ago. Did his leaving give her time to reconsider? Leo wouldn't blame her, but he sure as hell hoped nothing had changed.

He let himself into the darkened house, disappointment flaring that Poppy hadn't waited up. As if she owed him anything. Maybe he should have stayed at his own house for the night so he didn't bother her.

That would have given him the distance to try to loosen the bond he felt with her—the need that pounded through him whenever they were together. If he was being honest, it wasn't just when they were together.

This house had cast a spell on him. He felt pulled back any time he was away and the welcoming interior had quickly become a haven from the pressure of the outside world. Or maybe it wasn't the house at all but the woman who occupied it.

For a man who prided himself on his ability to have relationships with women without committing to anything more than a good time, all of his resolve dissipated when he was here with Poppy and Joey.

The closeness and something of their enmeshed lives filled his heart in a way he hadn't known he needed or could experience. And he could no more stay away than a magnet could resist the pull of its mate. He'd return as long as she let him, and he would force himself to be satisfied with whatever she was willing to give, whether or not it differed from what he wanted.

Quietly walking down the hall toward the spare bedroom, he felt his pulse leap as he noticed the light spilling out from the partially closed door of Poppy's room.

He knocked softly, and she beckoned him in, much to his relief. He'd never been in her bedroom before and she kept the door closed most of the time. Her citrusy scent filled the house, but it was stronger here. He wanted to rush to her bed and bury his nose in the pillow beside her. Bury himself in Poppy as the desire he'd falsely believed he could control pounded through him in another wave.

"A good night?" she asked, and something in her tone made his gaze sharpen on her. Her pajama shirt buttoned down the front with little panda faces covering it. Pandas were *not* sexy, he reminded himself, but his body was not getting the message. She sat propped up on overstuffed pillows, a book in her lap, but the smile she gave him didn't reach her eyes.

"I'm sorry I'm home so late," he said automatically, out of character for him. Leo made a habit of not apologizing, but he didn't like to think that the evening he'd spent at his mother's house was upsetting to Poppy.

"You don't owe me anything." There was an edge of disappointment in her voice. "I know you have your own life."

"My grandfather was in a restless mood, and I can tell it's taking a toll on my mom." He took a tentative step forward, almost expecting her to send him away.

She looked like a sleepy golden queen on a king-size throne. He wondered how many times a man had shared that bed with her, then mentally shook his head. None of his business, but he couldn't seem to tamp down the part of him that wanted it to be.

"I'm sure she appreciated you staying to take some of the weight off her shoulders. I know I do." She nodded toward the baby monitor on the dresser. "Leave yours off tonight," she told him. "I'll listen for the baby."

"It's my turn."

"Everybody gets a night off sometimes."

Why did she have to be so damn easygoing? Effortless to appreciate, like the first bite of a perfectly baked birthday cake.

"How was the night here?" He continued approaching the bed until he could sit down on the edge of it. She shifted her legs to make room for him. Always so accommodating.

"He took a full bottle, had a blowout diaper and several man-size burps."

Her smile widened as he chuckled. "I'm taking that as a sign it's going to be a restful night for all of us."

She nodded, then glanced down at the lavender duvet cover. Placing a hand on her covered leg, he gently traced the outline of her delicate ankle bone. "We started something earlier…"

"We did." She sounded breathless, and his body grew heavy, but he continued the light touch through the soft fabric without meeting her gaze.

"Then I got called away, which might be for the best." He forced a smile. "I'm sure it gave you time to change your mind about anything more."

"It did," she agreed, and it felt like his heart stopped. He glanced up at her, and the heat in her sea-green eyes stole his breath. "But I didn't change my mind."

"Poppy," he rasped. "Do you mean that?"

She nodded and sat forward, pressing a tentative kiss to his mouth. "More than you know."

It felt like his birthday and Christmas and the Fourth of July all rolled into one. Leo didn't understand his reaction. They were agreeing to sex, nothing more, but it was difficult to pull his thoughts together when his need for this woman overwhelmed everything else.

He placed his hands on either side of her face and angled her head to deepen the kiss, but she broke away.

"Is that a move?" she demanded, her voice trembling slightly.

"Excuse me?" He tried to make sense of her question.

"You cupping my cheeks like that. Do you do that with all the women you kiss?"

It was the strangest question he'd ever been asked, but he didn't say that. "No," he told her, which wasn't a lie. As experienced as he was with women, Leo couldn't remember ever wanting to simply hold and touch anyone other than Poppy. Hell, he'd be satisfied to spend all night kissing her.

"What happens between us is only about us, Poppy. You do something to me I can't explain, but it's undeniable. You are so special."

"*We* are special," she countered, and he wanted to believe her.

Leo didn't argue, although he was still convinced Poppy held the magic. He kissed her again, and when he couldn't seem to get close enough, he shifted until he was kneeling over her on the bed. She lay back against the pillow and wrapped her arms around his shoulders, her fingers tickling the hair at the nape of his neck.

Then she tugged on the hem of his sweater, and he happily yanked it over his head, feeling satisfaction rush through him at the way her eyes dilated as she splayed her open palms across his bare chest. He still wanted more. He wanted to feel her skin. She must have read his mind because she reached for her own shirt, leaning up to pull it over her head.

Heaven help him, she wasn't wearing a bra. It wasn't as if he'd never seen breasts before but viewing Poppy's body after spending an embarrassing amount of hours imagining it felt like a revelation.

He leaned in and licked the tip of one pink peak, gratified at her answering moan. Then forced himself to focus on the moment and not on the fact that it felt like he was floating on a cloud of desire he'd never before experienced.

It was a joy to take his time exploring her delectable

body despite the need of his own. Her skin was soft and smelled like summer, fresh and vibrant but mixed with a sinfully salty musk he knew came from her center.

He was both terrified he would lose control and determined to make this night the best she'd ever had.

She responded to every touch, every lick and tug, like they were exactly how she wanted to be ravished.

Her hands kneaded his back as she drew him closer, and he reached between them under the covers, expecting to find the hem of her pajama pants, and thrilled when the lacy corner of her panties was the only material to greet him. He groaned her name as he dipped two fingers inside her, finding her as ready for him as he felt.

Still, he took his time, mimicking with his tongue the movements of his fingers until Poppy gasped and broke apart underneath him. It was the most satisfying moment of Leo's life.

After one long, lingering kiss, he climbed off the bed. Shock registered in Poppy's eyes, but he held up a hand.

"I'm not going anywhere, sweetheart," he told her. "Unless you're finished with me?"

Her eyes tracked to the obvious erection straining the front of his jeans. "Nowhere near finished," she reassured him.

He got undressed and took a condom from his wallet and stretched it over his length. He joined Poppy on the bed again, rolling the two of them so that she was on top.

"Are you sure?" she whispered.

"Absolutely," he answered without hesitation. "This is the best view I could imagine." He just about died of happiness when she lowered herself onto him, taking every inch like she might never let go.

Her hips began to move, and he gripped her, a groan escaping his mouth. She was perfect, and he loved witnessing this new facet of her personality. Wild, free and not self-conscious about setting a pace that would ensure her pleasure was just as much of a priority as his.

Release found her again, and as she slumped forward on top of him, he flipped her so that her back was against the mattress. Then he plunged deep within her. She let out a muffled cry of satisfaction and met him thrust for thrust until he followed her over the edge.

Normally, this was where things got awkward for Leo. He didn't do the afterglow part so well. But just like everything else, being with Poppy made it different. Better. *Perfect.*

He forced himself to disentangle himself from her long enough to clean up and dispose of the condom before returning to the bed. She was just leaning over the side to reach for her pajama shirt.

"You won't need that." He lifted the covers on the other side and scooted toward her. "I'll keep you warm tonight."

For all the nights she would have him, he realized with a start. Even that awareness didn't scare him. Nothing could burst the bubble of contentment he was reveling in at the moment. Poppy snuggled closer, and he drew her tight into his embrace, drifting off with a smile on his face.

Chapter Eight

Leo woke the following day to the scent of coffee brewing and a cold, empty place in the bed beside him. Joey had only cried once during the night, and when Poppy started to get up, Leo had dropped a kiss on her forehead and told her to stay put.

He'd fed the sleepy baby a bottle, burped him and changed a wet diaper, re-swaddled the little guy, then put him down again. When Joey sighed and dropped back to sleep, Leo had the sensation of doing something remarkable with his life.

Although this arrangement had started out as a way to appease his grandfather's doubt about his character, Leo truly enjoyed taking care of Joey. And he felt like a good partner to Poppy, something that would have his previous girlfriends cackling in disbelief.

Wait. Was Poppy his *girlfriend*? Did he want her to be?

He hadn't put a label on a relationship since high school, and back then, it hadn't meant anything to him.

But what happened between them last night seemed significant. As if it meant more than he usually allowed sex to represent. It felt as though they'd made love.

No, no, no. Leo was not a naive teenager. He knew one didn't equal the other. That was why he'd implemented a rule as soon as he'd moved to his house: he never invited a woman to spend the night and didn't allow himself to sleep in someone else's bed.

Rules kept him safe. Especially his no relationship rule—the one that had wrecked his relationship with Poppy the first time around before they'd even gotten to the good stuff. But he was different now, or at least this arrangement felt different. Because he couldn't truly change, could he?

He needed to stop overthinking things. Otherwise, he'd do something stupid like bolt out the door and ruin everything. They'd made no promises to each other, and that's how it would stay. Without promises, he wouldn't risk hurting her. Or being hurt in return.

He'd put on his boxers at some point in the night after making lo—nope, *having sex* with Poppy for the second time. And while he should be sated, need rose in him again. Padding down the hall to his bedroom, he focused on the image of his third-grade math teacher, a terrifying woman with bony cheeks, a hooked nose and the scent of sauerkraut constantly wafting from her pores like she'd bathed in the stuff.

Okay, that helped get him under control. He pulled on sweatpants and a T-shirt and made his way to the kitchen. Joey sat in his bouncy chair on the counter, staring at the toy bar above him. Humphrey got up from his bed in front of the window and greeted Leo with an enthusiastic head butt.

Poppy came around the corner from the laundry room,

buttoning up a pair of jeans as she walked, then stopped at the sight of Leo.

"Why do you look guilty?" he blurted.

"I don't."

She definitely did.

She grabbed a ponytail holder from the catchall basket on the counter and tied back her hair. "What would I have to be guilty about? Do *you* feel guilty?"

"I feel fantastic," he said honestly. "Or at least I did. Where are you going?"

"I got a text a few minutes ago. My mom called another emergency family meeting."

He moved toward her for a good-morning kiss but seeing her tense up, changed course and headed for the coffee maker. What the hell was going on?

Never in a million years would he have guessed Poppy to be the one to put the postcoital distance between them. That was his role.

"She didn't give you any indication why?"

Poppy shook her head and then placed a hand on her stomach. "The message was vague and went out to my brothers and me, but there was something in the tone of it. I have a bad feeling."

Leo poured himself a cup and reached into the refrigerator for the creamer. "Do you think the rest of the DNA results came in?"

She looked sick at the thought, and he felt the same. A positive match would mean they'd know more—not only the identity of Joey's father but who his mother might be based on his dad's dating history. It also meant that this little interlude of playing house with no repercussions for the future might end just when it was getting really good.

"It's going to be okay, Poppy. No matter what happens."

She dashed a hand across her cheek as she stared at Joey. "I wish I could believe that."

Leo placed his mug on the counter and moved toward her. He barely recognized this version of himself—the one who wanted to comfort someone to ease their worry and pain. He didn't like complicated anything but especially emotions.

Ignoring all of his normal instincts, he wrapped his arms around her. She stood ramrod straight for a few seconds, then melted against him. His heart pinched with emotion, and he wanted to stay like this for as long as she'd have him.

"You must regret getting involved in this." She sniffed. "With me."

"Not for a second." He pulled back and kissed the center of her forehead, much as he had before falling asleep last night, tangled in each other's arms. "Go to your meeting. Joey and I will be here when you get back."

She shook her head. "You need to get to the vineyard. I'm sure yesterday's issues didn't disappear like a miracle."

"They can wait." He kissed her again. "Go ahead, Poppy. Trust me. I've got you."

"Thank you again," she said softly, her cheeks coloring as she added, "For last night, too."

His heart swelled, and he forced his features to remain neutral even though he wanted to jump for joy. "Anytime," he said with a wink. "I aim to please."

She frowned slightly but didn't comment on how much he sounded like a wanker.

After she left, Leo downed his coffee then lifted Joey into his arms. "You might not realize this," he told the boy, "but I used to be chill when it came to women. Any tips on how to reclaim it?"

The baby shoved his fist into his mouth.

"A man of few words." Leo nodded and poured himself another cup. "Good advice, kid. I'll remember it."

To Poppy's surprise, she was the last member of her family to enter the kitchen. Her mom and dad stood on opposite ends of the large island like they were facing off in some sort of high-noon shoot-out. The winter sun poured in through the bank of bay windows behind the table, but a heavy shadow seemed to hang over the room.

She'd never seen her parents at odds this way, and her stomach tightened painfully.

"You don't even recognize the number," Garth shouted.

"Don't raise your voice to me," Shelley answered in a harsh whisper.

Rafe and Shane stood just inside the doorway to the kitchen, both dressed for work in jeans, denim shirts and well-worn boots, watching their parents with twin looks of consternation.

"What's going on?" Poppy asked.

Her mother turned and Poppy had to stifle a gasp. Shelley's eyes were bloodshot and red-rimmed, her usual rosy complexion devoid of color. She looked absolutely miserable.

"I received a text early this morning," Shelley said, her voice hollow.

"From an anonymous number," Garth grumbled.

"It said your dad is Joey's father."

Rafe let out a string of curses while Shane shook his head. "How is that possible?" he asked no one in particular.

"That's what I want your father to explain." Shelley jabbed a finger in Garth's direction.

"It's *not* possible," their father said simply, but Poppy could see the lines of tension bracketing his mouth.

"What about the DNA test results?" Rafe stepped forward, hands fisting at his sides. "What is the holdup? Have you—"

Garth ran a shaking hand through his thick salt-and-pepper hair. "I called the supervisor of the testing lab this morning. I woke him up only to have him tell me they discovered late yesterday that the samples from me, your uncle and Micah haven't been reported because they're missing."

"They *lost* them?" Poppy moved toward her mother's side, but Shelley flinched away as if she couldn't stand to be touched.

"He gave me some line about the vandalism and theft and how crowded the lab is. His staff is scouring the place but..." Her father frowned and then met Poppy's gaze across the island. "I'm not that boy's father."

Shane strode toward their dad and placed a firm hand on his shoulder. "Keep it together. The three of you can give new DNA samples. We know you aren't—"

"We don't know anything." The words left Shelley's mouth in a staccato rhythm like bullets raining down on their close-knit family.

Growing up, Poppy had heard stories about other

branches of the illustrious Fortune family and the scandals and drama that had plagued certain members. As a girl, she'd lamented the boring normalcy of her own family. Even though her dad and uncle didn't get along, there had never been anything more than petty squabbles or veiled barbs thrown back and forth.

Now she realized a person should never wish for excitement in the form of scandal. It might be entertaining to an outsider but living it and dealing with the raw emotion made her chest feel like it was about to rip open. Her mother's anger, sadness and devastation were almost tangible, a bubble of upset surrounding Shelley that Poppy didn't know how to pierce.

Like her brothers, she never imagined her father would be associated with the baby in her care, even if some anonymous tipster offered up the unproven revelation. It must be some sort of mistake or misunderstanding. She had to believe her parents would get through this. They were strong. They loved each other.

"I'm moving out." Shelley audibly swallowed like the words left a sickening taste in her mouth.

"No." Garth shook his head and started around the island, but Shane held him fast. "You can't leave, Shel."

"Mom, you don't mean that!" Poppy lifted a hand toward her mother and then pulled it back because when Shelley turned to Poppy, she could see the resolve in her mother's gaze. The eyes that were usually filled with kindness and understanding had taken on a hard, bright glint.

"You can stay with me for a couple of days," Rafe offered, and they all ignored the hiss of displeasure that elicited from their father.

"I'm going to the Emerald Ridge Hotel in town." Shelley made a sharp movement with her hand when her husband would have protested. "I need space, Garth. I need time and I need answers. Until I get them, I'm staying at Emerald Ridge."

Poppy waited for her father to rage or argue. He wasn't a violent man, but he also didn't exactly have an inside voice at the best of times. His jaw remained clenched as he stared, devastated, at his wife of over three decades. He gripped his forehead between his thumb and index finger.

Poppy could imagine the pounding headache he must be trying to massage away. If it rivaled hers, no painkiller in the world would alleviate it.

Without a word, he turned on his heel and stomped out of the kitchen toward the back of the house.

Shane and Rafe exchanged a look then turned toward their mother. "Go on," Shelley told them. "I'm fine."

Neither brother looked like he believed her, but they followed Garth out of the room.

Shelley immediately sank onto one of the plush leather barstools. "I'm *not* fine," she whispered and Poppy enveloped her mom in a tight hug.

"It's not Dad," Poppy insisted. "He wouldn't do that to you. He loves you so much, Mom."

Shelley's shoulders trembled as she cried softly against Poppy's chest. Could a heart break in sympathy for someone else's pain? If so, hers was close to cracking in two. She didn't allow herself to cry, however, knowing she needed to be strong for her mom at that moment.

She didn't say anything else but held Shelley tight. The kitchen looked the same as it always did: bright, warm and welcoming, except for the cloud of sorrow that hung in the air. How was it possible that the baby who brought so much joy into Poppy's life was also the catalyst for this overwhelming pain that threatened to rip her family apart? Not that anyone blamed sweet Joey. He was innocent but still a reminder of a potential betrayal that would change all of them going forward.

It took several minutes before her mother's tears ebbed. Shelley pulled back and offered her a watery smile. "Where did you learn to hug like that?"

"My mom taught me." Poppy grabbed a wad of tissues from the box on the counter. "She's the best."

Shelley drew in a shaky breath and blew her nose. "Where's the baby?" she asked as if just now realizing Poppy didn't have him with her.

"Leo offered to stay home with him."

Her mother's lips thinned. "I'm still not sure how I feel about him staying with you."

"He's a huge help."

"He's also not a man who wants commitment."

"I know that," Poppy insisted. Despite the pleasure they'd shared last night, she also knew a roll in the sheets—even an amazing one—wouldn't change who a man was on the inside.

"Be careful," her mom said. "Look at me. I'm proof you're never too old for a broken heart."

"Let me see the text." Poppy held out her hand. Shelley unlocked the home screen then gave the phone to her.

"It's a Dallas area code," Poppy murmured, unnerved by the cryptic message.

"Your father tried to trace the number. Apparently, whoever sent it used a burner phone."

Poppy blinked. She would never have expected to hear her mother use the term *burner phone* except when talking about the details of a crime podcast she was bingeing.

"Mom, you don't have to go to the hotel. This house is plenty big enough if you need space."

"I don't want to be in the same house as your father right now."

"Then stay with me," Poppy suggested. "Leo would probably be thrilled at a break from baby duty." She didn't necessarily believe that and hoped it wasn't true. He'd never given her a reason to think he wanted out of their arrangement. If last night and this morning were any indication, he was all in—at least temporarily. But if her mom needed a place to stay...

Shelley rose from the chair and plucked a tall glass out of the cabinet, filling it with water then taking a long drink. "Your father and I wanted to shield you kids from this, but I've been contemplating a temporary separation for a while now."

Poppy felt her mouth drop open. If her mother had said she was running off to join the circus, it couldn't have been more of a surprise.

"Why?" she demanded, trying not to sound like a petulant kid. "You and Dad are happy. You love each other."

She sank into the chair her mother had just vacated as Shelley traced a finger around the rim of her glass, refusing to look up. "We do love each other, but it's more complicated. At least it is after all these years."

Poppy gripped the edge of the granite counter. "Did he cheat on you? Do you have proof?"

Her mother's delicate brows furrowed as a quiver ran

through her. Poppy hated everything about this conversation. Hated this morning that tipped the stability of her family like a toddler knocking over a stack of blocks.

"I have no proof he's cheating on me, and he denies it just like he denies the truth of the anonymous text." Shelley placed the now empty glass into the sink. "I hope time proves he's telling the truth, but your dad and I have hit a rough patch. Sometimes it happens, sweetheart. We've been together for a long time. It's not exactly fair that men are seen as distinguished and more attractive as they age and women..." She lifted her shoulders in a resigned shrug. "We just get old."

"Mom, no." Poppy climbed off the stool and went to hug her mother again. "You are beautiful. More beautiful than you were when you were young."

Her mother laughed and kissed Poppy's cheek. "My darling girl, I'm not complaining. I wouldn't trade my age for youth if someone offered to pay me, but there's no denying the truth." She released a quavering breath. "Please don't worry about me. Things will work out as they are meant to. Your father and I love you and your brothers. Even though it would be an adjustment, if the new test results show that Joey is a part of this family, I'll welcome him into it."

Poppy blinked away the tears that flooded her eyes. "I'm so sorry. I never thought having Joey here would be so difficult for you." She forced herself to continue, "If you need me to call the caseworker and find him a diff—"

"Of course the baby will stay with you. He's innocent, and more than anything, he deserves to be taken care of. No one can care for him better than my daughter. I know that."

There was a crash from the back of the house and Shelley winced. "I'm going to pack. I know this is hard on you in particular. The hopeless romantic in the family." She blew out a breath. "But it's what I need to do. I hope you'll support me."

"I'll always support you, Mom, just like you support me. Do you want help packing?"

"I can manage it. Go be with Joey. Give him an extra tight hug. Tell that Leonetti boy we appreciate his help. You can leave out the part where I have my doubts about him. It's more important to know that you aren't alone."

"Neither are you, Mom." After one final hug, Shelley went upstairs, and Poppy returned to her house.

She parked in the garage but walked outside to look up at the pale blue sky and the clouds floating on the breeze like they didn't have a care in the world.

Lucky clouds.

She turned at the sound of a door shutting. Leo stepped out of the garage. "I heard you come back and wanted to make sure everything was okay since you didn't come in right away." His face darkened as he studied hers. "Everything is not okay." The words were a statement rather than a question.

"It's terrible." A sob escaped her mouth. Her knees gave way and she started to crumple to the ground, but Leo caught her before she did.

"I think my parents are splitting up," she managed through her tears. It was stupid to react this way. She wasn't a kid anymore, and this separation might be temporary. But knowing her mom and dad didn't have the perfect marriage she'd believed rocked Poppy to her core.

If her parents couldn't make it work, what chance did anyone else have?

"They'll be all right," Leo said as he carried her into the house. "You'll be all right, Poppy."

She buried her head in his shoulder and inhaled the spicy, sexy scent of him. "I can walk," she protested but didn't make any move to wiggle out of his arms.

"I know, but this is an excuse to get my hands on you again."

His teasing helped to calm the chaotic emotions still coursing through her. He didn't stop until he was at the sofa. Even when he sat, he continued to cradle her in his arms. She didn't try to move away but took the comfort he offered.

"Tell me as much or as little as you want," he said. "If you want to be left alone, I understand that, too, and—"

"I don't," she quickly replied. The thought of being alone at the moment felt unbearable. She explained the text, her father's reaction and her mother's insistence on moving to town. Leo seemed shocked by this new development.

"It will work out," he assured her. Even though he had no way of knowing that, his words soothed her.

"The worst part is the lab losing the DNA samples." She squeezed shut her eyes. "My father can't prove his innocence without them."

Leo considered that for a few weighted seconds before he answered. "Are you still convinced he's innocent?"

She started to nod, offended that he'd make the suggestion then stopped. At this point, she couldn't be certain of anything.

"It's what I want to believe that counts."

He pulled her close again, but she could hear his phone buzzing from the counter.

"You need to go," she whispered.

He nodded. "I wish I could spend the whole day just holding you."

She sighed and climbed off his lap. "It's okay. I appreciate everything you've done already."

He didn't release her hand. "Come with me," he said.

"To the vineyard?"

She'd heard amazing things about the property Leo and his family owned on the other side of town and had recommended it to clients looking for a local winery experience, but he'd hadn't taken her there when they'd dated years earlier. And then after it ended she didn't want to run into him and take the chance of it being awkward. And speaking of awkward...

"Won't it be weird with your mom and grandfather?"

Leo chuckled and kissed her knuckles. "My grandfather has been begging me to bring you to see him. Mom will love it. She adores babies. My nieces are the light of her life."

Poppy swallowed as emotion caught in her throat. "My mom loves babies, too. She's such a good grandmother to Brady and also Rafe's daughter before the accident. It's hard for her with Joey and everything we don't know about him. The possibility that..." She broke off.

"It's understandable." He stood and wrapped an arm around her shoulder. "This is a difficult situation for your family and the missing test results only make it more so. Can they spare you at the spa today?"

"I think so. It's busy this week but I can make the time."

Leo gave her a grin so boyishly pleased she couldn't help but return it. "Prepare to be dazzled by your own private vineyard tour, Poppy."

"What about Joey?"

"He'll come with us. There are photos of me in my father's arms in the field the day I came home from the hospital."

Poppy nodded, even though it wasn't the same. As much as she wanted to pretend they were family, Leo wasn't Joey's father. She might not be the baby's foster mother for much longer. That made her even more committed to relishing the time she did have with the two of them.

"I'll head over now and finish up the work I can't put off. Joey's been down for about a half hour so he shouldn't sleep much longer. Text when you're on your way and we'll meet at the winery office."

He leaned in to give her another long, lingering kiss before grabbing his wallet and phone from the counter.

Poppy listened to the sound of his car driving away as she snuggled Humphrey, who'd ambled over to keep her company in Leo's absence.

It might not be the most prudent decision, but she intended to enjoy everything Leo was willing to give her before their time together ended. She might not know what her future held, but she'd savor all the happiness she could manage along the journey.

Chapter Nine

"Are you nervous about your girlfriend coming for a visit?"

Leo tried to ignore his youngest sister, much as he would a gnat flying near his face.

But Gia wouldn't be snubbed so easily. She danced around him in the winery's tasting room, chanting "Leo's got a girlfriend" like she was an annoying little kid.

Deep down he hoped Poppy would love the tasting room the way he did. Leo had always found the interior to be warm and welcoming to visitors, with rich wood trim and tall windows that allowed the tasting tables and counter to be bathed in light for hours each day. The shelves and glass cases showcased the winery's chosen varietals, while cushioned chairs and sofas invited guests to enjoy their visit. He wanted Poppy to appreciate every aspect.

"Poppy is a *friend*," he said when he couldn't take the chorus any longer. He was standing near the front window so he'd see when she pulled up. His mom and grandpa were at the main house as far as he knew but he had no intention of taking the chance that they might walk over to greet her on their own.

"You've never brought a *friend* who's a girl to the vineyard," Gia pointed out as if that meant something.

"Have you always been this irritating?"

"Yes," she answered without hesitation. "It's my role as the baby of the family."

"At least I only have you to deal with today." He blew out a breath, still surprised by the nerves flitting through his gut. Bella and Antonia had driven down to Dallas with Bella's kids for the day.

"Trust me, I have orders to report back on everything." She patted him on the arm. "We're taking credit for this, you know."

"For what?"

She grinned. "For you and Poppy. You clearly took our advice and figured out how to put all of that Leo Leonetti charisma to good use for once. Rizzing up Poppy Fortune."

"That's not what's happening," he said through gritted teeth. It would be much easier to understand if it was just a matter of charm or charisma. He knew how to wield both, but things with Poppy felt different in a way that confounded him.

Mostly because his actions with her came from his heart, which seemed intent on leading him to places his brain warned were dangerous.

"She's dealing with a lot right now, and I'm trying to support her." He shrugged at the skeptical look his sister leveled at him. "I'm not thinking about *rizzing up* anyone."

Gia surprised him by wrapping her arms around his waist. "I'm so proud of you," she said against his chest. "I can't wait to get to know Poppy. She always seems so nice, but I've only talked to her briefly at the FGR spa. She must be special for you to change so much."

"I haven't changed that much," he grumbled. "It's not like I was some womanizing ogre before this."

Gia released him and chuckled. "No one would describe you as an ogre."

He noticed she failed to address his womanizing comment and didn't like what that said about him or the prevailing opinion he knew most people, including his family, had about his character.

What would they think when his time with Poppy came to an end? What would *he* feel?

She pulled into the gravel parking lot, and he pushed aside those disturbing thoughts. Leo preferred to concentrate on *not* feeling. His attention was best left dedicated to the family business.

"Don't make this weird," he commanded his sister. "You stay here and…"

Gia was already rushing from the tasting room toward the winery's front entrance. Leo hustled to catch up with her. He exited the building and met Poppy's gaze over Gia's shoulder as his sister embraced her like they were long-lost friends.

Even though he'd instructed his sister not to make things weird, it was—as always—Poppy's ability to adapt to any situation that ensured the encounter didn't become awkward.

She accepted the youngest Leonetti's enthusiastic embrace and happily answered Gia's rapid-fire questions about Joey, the latest specials at the spa and the foster kittens Leo had told his family about over dinner last week.

He had to give Gia credit. For all of her inability to employ personal boundaries, the one subject she didn't go near was the mystery surrounding Joey's parents.

His sister gleefully took Joey from Poppy's arms. After cooing over the baby and peppering his forehead with kisses for several minutes, she handed him to Leo and excused herself to return to the tasting room, where a tour was scheduled to begin.

"I'm sorry for that," Leo said when they were alone again. "To be honest, I was more worried about my grandfather overwhelming you. But Gia ripped the too-much-too-soon bandage right off."

Poppy squeezed his hand, and he took the opportunity to link their fingers together. "She's adorable. I already feel ten times lighter than I did this morning. Thank you for inviting me into your world for a little bit."

For as long as you want in, he wanted to tell her but didn't because that was an emotional check he didn't think his heart could cash.

"The most impressive part of this place is the vines," he said, leading her toward the Polaris Ranger ATV. "Bella is the vintner. She has a gift with the grapes, but everyone in my family loves them in our own way."

Poppy let out a sigh. "That's how my brothers, cousins and I feel about the ranch. My cousins might run the cattle operation, but we all take part at different times. At least once a year, we do a family night at the spa."

Leo laughed. "Somehow, I can't see Rafe getting a facial."

"You'd be surprised." Poppy adjusted Joey's cap. "My brother rocks the clay mask like nobody's business."

"No way."

"Don't knock it." Poppy turned to him, pretending to examine his skin. "One of these nights, I'll give you a facial. I got my aesthetician's license a few years ago so I can fill in during the busier times."

"I would love that."

Her eyes sparkled at his response like he'd surprised her. It shocked the hell out of him, but Poppy's dedication to work and family and their legacy was another thing he loved about—no, *admired* about her, he amended silently.

He'd already moved the baby's car seat base and infant carrier from his truck to the back seat of the off-road vehicle, and the boy fell asleep as soon as the engine revved.

Poppy glanced toward Joey and then at Leo. "I worried the noise and vibration would upset him."

Leo put the vehicle into gear and started toward the vineyard. "Gia was like that as a baby. The motion and noise put her right to sleep every time. I remember Mom piling us into one of the old vineyard four-wheelers to drive up and down all over the property so my baby sister would take a nap."

Poppy looked around the vehicle's interior then rapped her knuckles on her head. "Knock on wood that Joey stays a good sleeper."

"We'll deal with whatever he throws our way," he told her. Leo felt like he could do anything with this incredible woman beside him, driving on the lush, fertile land that had been in his family for generations.

"This is already the best day I've had in a long time." Poppy placed her hand on top of his on the gearshift, and Leo's heart swelled.

"You're going to love the vineyard," he promised and to his surprise the word *love* rolled right off of his tongue.

To his relief, Poppy didn't react like it meant something more, and he settled in to share with her the part of his life he'd never shown to anyone else.

Poppy knew her family was unique. The fact that two generations of Emerald Ridge Fortunes lived and worked on the ranch that had been a part of their family for nearly a century made them noteworthy in this part of the state.

However, the Leonettis took close-knit to a new level, their pride in the vineyard and their Italian heritage on full display around the property and in the family home.

At FGR, the two families had always remained somewhat separate as they went about daily life. Poppy and her brothers had only grown closer to their cousins since Rafe and Drake had conceived and launched the Gift of Fortune program. However, the love and affection between the members of Leo's family felt natural and long-standing.

It was inspiring to tour the property with Leo; his passion for both winemaking and running the business side of the operation was infectious. Every employee greeted him with a mix of affection and admiration, a testament to how much he meant to his staff. She'd had no idea the amount of planning, strategy and cooperation from Mother Nature it took to make a vineyard successful.

After the tour, they'd returned to the tasting room, where she'd expected his youngest sister to join them as Leo poured samples of some of his favorite vintages. The depth of his knowledge astonished her even though she understood his family history with the vineyard. During their talks, Leo typically gave more credit to his family for the winery's success and took little for himself. Poppy understood his dedication in a deeper way and was thrilled by his encouragement as she attempted to identify the different notes in the vintages.

Gia joined them again, and to Poppy's surprise, reported that the other two sisters had returned home. Along with Leo's mom and grandfather and Antonia's baby, they were waiting at the main house. She looked a little sheepish explaining that as much as they wanted to visit with Poppy, all of them, including Bella's two kids, were most excited to get their hands on little Joey. She'd asked if she could take the bundled-up boy who'd woken from his nap to the house while they took their time with the tasting.

Poppy's face flushed when Gia made a point of telling Leo that the rest of the staff had been sent home for the night, and she was locking the door on her way out.

"Does your sister think you need help getting lucky?"

"That would be a first," Leo had answered with a wink. "But she's currently my favorite sister because of it."

Without another word, he picked her up and carried her into his office, where they made love on the leather sofa. He'd proved himself as attentive and thorough in worshipping her body as he'd been the night before.

The time before her mom had received that awful text felt like a world away, but this afternoon gave her the distance she needed to regain her composure after the events of this morning. She once again felt certain her family would be okay—just like her mother said.

* * *

"You have a fine boy here, Poppy," Leo's grandfather said as he cradled the baby. Martina set out a delicious charcuterie for the group to snack on.

The Leonettis took turns holding Joey, all of them doting on the baby, and it made her once again wish that whoever Joey's parents were, they wouldn't be related to her. In truth, she hoped the mystery might remain unsolved and that she'd eventually be allowed to adopt the baby, who already felt like hers.

"I couldn't have managed so well without Leo," she admitted, and his grandfather beamed.

"I told him there's more to life than work," Enzo said, "but it took you and this tiny man to prove it."

Poppy glanced at Leo, who was sipping a glass of wine, his hip resting against the kitchen counter.

"Papa always knows best," he said lightly, although his gaze looked troubled.

Was it too much having them here with his family? She hoped the Leonettis wouldn't be too disappointed when things between them came to their inevitable end. As sad as that would make her, she knew she shouldn't allow herself to believe there was any other way. She'd opened her heart and had it broken on more than one occasion. Life had taught her that hope was a treacherous thing when it came to love.

Apparently, the lesson hadn't stuck because each day she spent with Leo, her heart opened to him more and more. It didn't feel like she had any power to stop it, and she was lying to herself if she believed otherwise. Lying to all of them—her family and his, which was a hard pill to swallow.

Poppy didn't like feeling as though they were deceiving people who cared about them, especially Enzo. But would it be so wrong for her to hold out hope that this time it could be different? Leo wasn't the same man he'd been during their first try at a relationship. Maybe he just needed someone to make him see that. She couldn't be that someone if she let herself.

"What are you guys doing for Valentine's Day?" Antonia, the quietest of three sisters, asked.

"Nothing," Poppy answered truthfully, realizing the holiday was in a few days.

Leo's mother gasped in dismay and pointed the fork she held in Leo's direction. "I raised you better than that. You must take a woman out on this important day that celebrates your love."

Leo looked like he wanted the floor to swallow him whole, which was exactly how Poppy felt.

"It's not a big deal," she told the group. "Dinner out isn't exactly an option with an infant."

"Of course not," his mother agreed. "Leo's grandfather and I will watch the baby."

"Do you hear that?" Enzo gently jiggled the boy, who continued to gaze up at him. "You and I will have another night together."

"A sleepover if you'd like," Martina offered.

Poppy held up her hands. "Oh, no. That's too much. You don't have to…"

She met Leo's gaze across the room, unable to read his expression.

"Poppy's right," he agreed after a moment. "It's a big ask and too late to make reservations. Valentine's Day is a fake holiday, anyway."

Gia and Antonia let out twin groans of disgust.

"That's something only an idiot would say." Bella reached across the center island and pinched her brother's arm. "Don't be an idiot."

He looked so discombobulated that Poppy almost laughed. Leo warned her his family had assumed that they were a couple because of his willingness to participate so fully in caring for Joey.

At first, she thought it was funny and knew certain members of her family probably believed the same, but now his shoulders slumped as his sisters and mother glared at him. She understood that he'd given up so much to be the man his family needed him to after his father died. The last thing she wanted was for their ruse to put more pressure on him or give his family false hope that more would come of their arrangement.

Except they could make it more. It would take time, but she had that and enough patience to allow Leo to see that they were good together. And it could be so much better if they opened their hearts. If she led by example on that front.

Enzo continued to stare down at the baby, even though Poppy had a feeling he was trying to refrain from laughing at the predicament his grandson faced.

That odd protectiveness she felt for Leo rose to the surface. "Leo and I agreed not to celebrate Valentine's Day." She made her tone firm as she met Bella's gaze. "I don't need a special holiday or night on the town to feel special. Your brother does that every day with how he supports me and cares for Joey."

She placed her hands on her hips. "Heck, he even

scoops the litter box, and when you're dealing with foster kittens, that can be a messy job."

There was a beat of stunned silence in the kitchen, then Bella asked, "Are you saying scooping poop is romantic?"

Poppy laughed. "I'm saying there are more-important ways to show you care about someone than a heart-shaped box of chocolates or overpriced roses."

She still couldn't read Leo's expression, but at least he stood a little bit taller. She'd done that for him. Given how much he'd helped her in the past few weeks, it was the least she could offer.

Before she knew what was happening, Martina wrapped her in a tight embrace. "You are a treasure," she told Poppy. "And you…"

Still gripping Poppy's arm, she pulled her toward Leo and gave her son a loud, smacking kiss on the cheek. "You make me so proud, Leonardo."

Poppy hadn't expected such an emotional reaction from Leo's mother and hoped he didn't mind her unprompted defense. He could handle himself, but for some reason, he didn't. Something held him back from owning who he was and the choices he made.

Maybe it was the pressure of being the oldest and only son. Poppy had been judged plenty over the years. Most people in town thought she was a silly romantic who must have some fatal flaw that made her incapable of keeping a man. Was she too needy? Too vulnerable? Too ordinary for anyone to truly cherish?

Any or all of those things might be true, but she'd decided she was also satisfied with who she was as a person on the inside. None of her doubts or fears or other people's judgments would control her life.

If she could give Leo one thing during their time together, it would be the ability to accept himself, and that would start with convincing his family to accept him and where he was in life.

Although if that were the case, letting them believe he had more interest in Poppy than was true wouldn't help matters He might be different than the man she'd dated, but that only meant he had more power to break her heart if she gave it to him.

But when he wrapped an arm around her waist and pulled her close and out of his mother's grasp, all she could do was enjoy the feel of his warmth against her body. For something that she knew wasn't real, it certainly felt that way.

"Will you be my valentine?" Leo asked, his breath tickling the hair around her ear. Her mouth went dry as desire sparked along her skin.

"Yes," she answered, kissing the edge of his jaw. His mom and sisters let out cheers of delight and Poppy blushed. She'd forgotten they had an audience because that's what Leo did to her. He made her forget everything, including her determination to keep her heart guarded.

Chapter Ten

A few days later, Leo dropped Joey off at his mother and grandfather's before returning to Poppy's house to pick her up for their evening of dinner and dancing in the ballroom at the Emerald Ridge Hotel. Leonetti Vineyards supplied much of the wine for the hotel so he'd called in a favor from the owner.

He'd never taken a woman out on Valentine's Day. All part of his determination not to set expectations he couldn't live up to. Deep in his cynical soul, a voice whispered that this was a huge mistake.

It didn't matter that he and Poppy both knew the terms of their arrangement, and she had never pushed or even hinted that she wanted more.

The problem originated inside him because, to his continued shock, he wanted to push. Over the years, he'd seen more than one friend worn down by a girlfriend only to end up in a long-term relationship, and in some cases, even marriage. Those poor fools seemed happy enough.

Maybe if Poppy forced him, he could commit without really capitulating, the way he did so often in his family. He bent to what they wanted and expected of him without having to take full responsibility for those decisions.

Yeah. That would be okay. Not forever. He wasn't marriage material even though he had trouble imagining his life without her. He'd learned from his father what committing to forever if you weren't ready would do to a person, but Leo couldn't imagine his life without Poppy and Joey in it so…

He gripped the bouquet he held in his hand—not overpriced roses—more tightly and walked into the house with a new sense of purpose.

Then came up short at the sight of Poppy standing in the entryway, shoving a tube of lipstick into the compact velvet purse she held.

"I haven't worn lipstick for weeks," she said. "I almost forgot how to apply the stuff." She pressed her lips together, drawing Leo's gaze. They were shaded in a soft plum color, darker than her natural pink and almost the same hue as they took on after he thoroughly kissed her.

His body urged him to chuck the flowers over his shoulder, forget about their dinner reservation and carry her back to the bedroom and peel that gorgeous dress right off her even more beautiful body.

The dress was amazing, or more accurately, she *looked* amazing in it. It was deep burgundy with a low V-neck that sorely tempted him to dip his tongue into the crevice between her breasts. The fabric clung to her hips and shimmered as she fidgeted in front of him.

"Is it too much? You're staring at me like it's too much."

He shook his head and opened his mouth, but no words came out. He couldn't breathe, let alone formulate a sentence.

A crease formed between her brows, and she drew

that plum-colored bottom lip between her upper teeth. "Too much," she whispered, possibly more to herself than him.

When she started to turn away, Leo got ahold of himself. He stepped forward and took her hand, linking their fingers together. She'd painted her nails. They reminded him of tiny rubies sparkling in the light from the fixture overhead. "You are never too much for me, Poppy."

One corner of her mouth lifted in an almost smile, but she didn't look convinced.

"You're so beautiful I lost my ability to speak. You take my breath away. There aren't words for what I feel when I look at you."

At least not words Leo would ever utter.

Thankfully, she didn't seem to need him to. Because of her heels, they were nearly the same height. She leaned in and brushed a featherlight kiss against his mouth. When he tried to deepen it, she pulled away.

"The disadvantage of lipstick." She used the pad of her thumb to wipe his lip. "You'll end up with more of it on your face than mine if we aren't careful."

"Worth it," he told her. "We won't need to worry if we skip dinner and—"

"Oh, no." She took another step back. "We're taking advantage of our babysitters and going out."

He saw the moment her doubts about the night crept in because a shadow entered her green eyes, turning them the color of the ocean just before a storm.

"Unless you're having second thoughts about—"

"Not one," he assured her. "I'm excited for no dish duty and even more to share a first dance with you."

The shadow cleared at his words, but she wrinkled her nose. "I'm not the best dancer."

"Sweetheart…" He leaned in like they were sharing a secret. "Dancing is an excuse to get my hands on you *in* that dress before I get my hands on you *out* of that dress. You'll do fine."

He was rewarded with an adorable blush and took her hand as he led her out the front door. Leo couldn't remember ever anticipating an evening so eagerly, especially not one that called for him to wear a sports coat and tie. But Poppy was exceptional, and he'd been an oaf when they'd tried dating a decade ago. This time it would be different. He'd do his best to make amends for the past and ensure this night was perfect for them both.

"Are people *still* staring?" Poppy asked, trying not to be obvious as she turned to glance at the patrons seated at the tables around them.

They'd been at Captains, the fancy restaurant on the top floor of the Emerald Ridge Hotel, for nearly two hours, and Poppy had enjoyed a delectable three-course meal of fresh ceviche, a perfectly blackened serving of Chilean sea bass and the most amazing crème brûlée she'd ever tasted for dessert.

Leo reached across the table and grasped her fingers. She started to tug them away, but he held fast, his smile never wavering.

"If they are, it's because you look as beautiful as you did when we walked in." He lifted her hand to his mouth, but she yanked it away.

"You can't do that here."

"Why not?" His voice was a low rumble.

"Everyone will think we're together."

He picked up the wineglass and swirled the dark liquid that complemented the color of her dress. It was a rich Syrah from his family's vineyard. "We *are* together. It's Valentine's Day, and we're on a date, in case you've forgotten. You also happen to look so gorgeous I *still* can't stop staring. Why would I care if people think we are together?"

Why would she expect him to understand? Leo didn't have the reputation in town that Poppy did. The polar opposite reputation, which meant no one would think twice about Leo on the date but Poppy...

"I told you I'm not doing relationships at the moment."

"And I'm okay with that," he agreed, although his eyes narrowed like he didn't like it.

"So when this ends, everyone will think I was a fool to give my heart again. They'll feel sorry for me. I'm tired of being pitied because I'm a failure at love."

She gripped the napkin tightly and ordered herself not to run from the table as embarrassment washed over her. Why was it so easy to share her most secret and humiliating thoughts with this man?

"We should have gone to dinner in the next town over," she muttered.

Leo studied her for what felt like hours, but it probably took only seconds before he said, "You aren't a failure at love. You have more love in your life, Poppy Fortune, than almost any person I know. The people you love are so lucky."

He shrugged, looking almost boyishly embarrassed. "I can hardly believe anyone would think I'm the kind of man who deserves you, but I'm proud as hell if they do. I'm grateful to be here, and I don't care what anybody assumes or what they say. When this ends, we can play it however you want. I'll be the one who's brokenhearted if that makes you happy. Please don't let what other people think or assume ruin this night."

Her heart first expanded at his words and then caved in on itself because amid all the flattery directed her way, he'd also used the phrase *when this ends*.

She didn't want it to end. Most of her worry was directed at her own heart because she couldn't stop falling for him. Leo had become the man she'd always wished him to be. A man who could fully capture her heart.

He might be willing to play at being crushed when they broke up, but Poppy knew she'd never be the same after this ended.

"You've changed," she murmured, and his wide-eyed expression told her he was as surprised as her that she'd made the observation out loud.

"Everyone changes," he answered, his voice tight.

"I like this version of you." Her voice sounded husky to her own ears and she cleared her throat. "I mean, I liked you five years ago but it's…different now."

An emotion flashed in his eyes that she couldn't name, but it made her pulse quicken. "Maybe we're both different."

"Maybe," she agreed, although one thing that hadn't changed is her attraction to Leo. It was only growing stronger the more time they spent together, and she was tired of resisting the way he pulled her in so effortlessly.

The waiter cleared their dinner plates just as the band took the stage. When the music started, a pretty decent cover of a popular love song by Adele, Leo stood. With a smile, he held his hand out to her.

"Ms. Fortune, may I have this dance?"

She hesitated, and his smile faltered. "Poppy?"

She shook off her worries, a task becoming more frequent and difficult each day. But it wasn't Leo's fault that she couldn't control her feelings. Tonight she'd find a way to enjoy how special he made her feel without worrying about the future. Or at least not worrying too much. That became easier as he led her to the dance floor, where a few couples were already swaying to the music.

"The moment I've been waiting for all night," he said as he pulled her close. He held her right hand, and she rested her left one on his shoulder as he began to lead her around the dance floor.

The first song was awkward. Poppy hadn't exaggerated when she'd told him she wasn't a good dancer, but Leo didn't so much as wince when she trod upon his toes. He simply pulled her closer and whispered, "Relax," against her ear.

To her shock, her body overrode her brain's swirling anxiety and did just that. Once she stopped thinking, she found it easier to enjoy the moment.

When was the last time she'd danced with a man? It had been at Rafe's wedding, with Poppy fresh off another breakup. She'd been chosen as a pity partner by her brothers and cousins. Eventually, she'd slunk into the shadows—hiding behind a potted palm—and watched the actual couples glide across the floor, wondering why relationships or even casual dating came so easy for other people but never for her.

Her parents had spent most of the evening dancing to everything from romantic ballads to country line dances. To Poppy, they'd seemed like the epitome of happiness, two people who'd found their perfect partner. Her chest pinched at the thought of what the future might hold for them and the role the baby who she loved with her whole heart would play in it.

As Leo smiled then twirled her so expertly, she felt as though their next stop was a standing ovation from the *Dancing with the Stars* judges. Poppy understood how deceiving looks could be. She and Leo might appear to fit together but their reality and eventual ending had the power to devastate her.

"You okay?" he asked, attuned to her emotions in a way that should be alarming but caused a thrill of happiness to flare in her heart.

She opened her mouth to tell him no. She *wasn't* okay. He couldn't come home with her again. There was no way she could continue to play the part of friends given how much she was coming to care for him. It went way beyond attraction, intoxicating as their physical connection could be. Her feelings far transcended gratitude for his help with Joey.

Leo was the crux of her emotions. She cared too deeply for him—for how he made her feel cherished and special. Like he saw her as something more than dependable, easygoing Poppy. He asked questions about her day like the answers mattered. Often, he solicited her opinion about issues he was dealing with at the winery, as if her ideas and suggestions offered a unique perspective, one that he respected and honored.

Although Poppy took her role in the FGR organization seriously, she often wondered if her parents, brothers and cousins did the same. She ran the spa and it made money and contributed to the reputation and success of the guest ranch arm of the business. But dealing with skincare products and pampering didn't often seem as significant as guest relations or supervising the cattle operation.

However, Leo helped her see that she mattered, and even though it might lead to heartbreak, she wasn't willing to give that up just yet. As this potential scandal with her parents proved, life had no guarantees. So even though her feelings became more tangled each day, she wanted to continue to enjoy whatever moments she and Leo had left. Despite the challenges, was it too much to hope this could be their second chance? And was she a fool for wanting it so badly?

"I'm fine." She lifted her hand to the back of his neck, loving his warm skin under her palm. Let people watch and talk. Poppy would savor the contentment that came with knowing she was the only woman this enigmatic man had let in. "Just a little tired."

His eyes closed when her nails grazed the skin above his starched collar. "Tired," he repeated in a whisper.

"Well, not exactly *tired* tired." His gaze felt like it pierced her soul with its intensity when he opened his eyes to stare into hers.

"What kind of tired?" He sounded hoarse like he had trouble forming the question. Another song had started, a fast dance number, but they stood still in the center of the dance floor, ignoring the couples who spun and whirled around them.

"Tired of not being alone with you." She flashed a cheeky smile and added, "Tired of not being naked."

Leo gave a choked response, then grabbed her hand and dragged her toward the ballroom's exit.

"My purse," she reminded him with a laugh.

"Don't move." He released her hand and sprinted to their table to retrieve her sparkly clutch, holding it tight to his chest like a football as he raced back to her and led her out into the quiet night.

"Heels," she protested when he started to pick up speed across the parking lot.

Barely breaking stride, Leo scooped her into his arms. He moved like a man possessed, and some of Poppy's doubts melted away with the intoxicating knowledge that this strong, handsome, confounding man might be as affected by her as she was by him.

Despite his frantic rush to the truck, Leo deposited her on the front seat like she was as delicate as a porcelain doll. He pulled the seat belt across her chest and lap, leaning in for a deep, soulful kiss as the buckle clicked.

Then he climbed in and started for her house, his knuckles white around the steering wheel.

He didn't speak, but Poppy could feel the desire pulsing between them. It glimmered in the air like diamonds. Her body throbbed with need, and it felt as though the ten-minute drive would be too much to bear. She'd explode with longing if they didn't...

"Leo?"

"Need to concentrate," he rasped.

"Leo, please." She reached out and placed a hand on his leg. He let out a hiss as his muscles bunched and then quivered.

"Poppy, I'm not sure I can."

"Take a right," she told him. "Now."

He didn't question her as he turned the truck onto the unmarked dirt road at the edge of the FGR property.

The truck's brights showed the open fields of sagebrush before them.

"There's a gate up ahead. No one except the ranch hands uses this entrance and only when they need to access one of the outer pastures. It's private."

His gaze flicked to hers, the question in them evident even in the dim glow from the dash.

"And close." She squeezed his leg. "Closer than home, and I can't wait." She wanted his hands on her skin, his mouth fused to hers.

The air sizzled between them as he turned off the engine, killed the lights and reached for her.

"That's the nicest thing anyone has ever said to me."

He threaded his fingers through her hair and leaned over the console to kiss her. Although the taste of him was familiar by now, she lost herself in the pleasure of it. Her body hummed with need and desire, and when he tugged her closer, she maneuvered herself onto his lap, straddling him. He moved the seat back, and they both laughed when she leaned into the horn.

"I feel like I'm back in high school," Leo confessed, trailing kisses along her neck. Her dress bunched around her hips, and he kneaded her bare skin with his fingers.

"I never did this in high school." She laughed self-consciously. "Clearly, I was missing out."

She'd never been confident enough to tell a man to pull over because she couldn't wait. Leo made her feel bold, and she wanted to revel in it.

"Tell me what you want." His voice was low and seemed to offer all sorts of wicked promises Poppy could barely acknowledge.

But she'd for sure try. "Touch me," she said, grateful for the darkness because she could feel the heat in her cheeks.

He gripped her legs, thumbs grazing the sensitive skin on the inside of her thighs. "Here?"

A moan escaped her lips.

"And here?" He leaned forward to run his tongue along her collarbone.

"No, not there," she managed, her breath coming in rasps.

His right hand scraped the fabric of her panties.

"Yes," she whispered.

Humming with approval, he dipped one finger inside her.

The horn blared again when she bucked backward. Leo chuckled and wrapped an arm around her.

"Easy," he told her then kissed her again.

It was easy to give herself over to the pleasure of his touch, the rhythm he set with his fingers and his mouth.

"So beautiful," he murmured against her mouth.

"More," she answered and barely recognized her own voice. Poppy had never demanded anything of anyone.

Leo didn't seem to mind. He deepened the kiss and his touch until she was mindless with sensation. Too much. It was *too much,* but he didn't stop. Her hips writhed in time with his fingers until she reached the peak and tumbled over the edge.

The darkness had no hold over her because her entire body felt like it was bathed in light. She threw back her head and called out his name, her voice echoing in the truck's cab.

And then the lights from the approaching truck hit her. She scrambled off Leo like she'd been electrocuted.

"Oh, my gosh." She twisted her dress into place as she turned to stare out the truck's back window. "No one comes down this road." She glanced at Leo. "Why are you grinning?"

"You're cute about being caught fooling around."

"Because I've never been caught!" She drew in a sharp breath. "Wait. What if whoever's in that truck is the person who's been sabotaging the ranches? It could be the villain."

Leo's smile dimmed. "Then we'll deal with it. I'll take care of you, Poppy. I promise."

She believed him, and her heart seemed to skip a beat. Leo reached out and linked their fingers as Poppy continued to watch the truck draw closer, exhaling in relief when she recognized the Fortune's Gold Ranch logo on the side. "It's one of our vehicles."

As the truck parked behind them, Leo turned on the engine. A man got out and approached the driver's side. Leo rolled down the window as Micah shone a flashlight into the cab.

"Poppy? Leo?" Her cousin frowned.

"What the hell are you two doing out here?"

Poppy's face flamed, but Leo remained cool. "Stargazing."

Micah looked between the two of them, and Poppy shrugged. "I've always loved the night sky, and it's so clear with no lights around. How did you know we were here?"

Her cousin flipped off the flashlight. "I installed game cams around the perimeter of the property. Can't take any more chances with the bad stuff happening lately."

"Sorry we bothered you," Leo said smoothly.

"I was just watching TV," Micah answered easily. "You won't find me venturing out on Valentine's Day."

Poppy rolled her eyes at that. "You sound like my brothers."

"Smart guys." Micah reached in to pat Leo's shoulder. "Not as smart as you taking out our Poppy. She's one of a kind."

"Yes, she is," Leo agreed brusquely. "And she's mine."

Micah grinned then winked at Poppy before heading back to his truck. "Enjoy the rest of the night."

"Let's go home, sweetheart." Leo grabbed her hand again and lifted it to his mouth. Instead of kissing her knuckles, he turned it over and pressed his mouth to the inside of her wrist. "We have a little time before we need to pick up Joey…"

She grinned. "Then let's make the most of it."

Chapter Eleven

Poppy entered Coffee Connection, her favorite coffee spot in town, two mornings later with Joey's infant carrier tucked under her arm.

It was the first time since the baby had come to live with her that she'd brought him into town on her own. Her staff and some of the regular clients at the spa had met him as he came to work with her if Leo was at the winery.

But the spa felt different than being in public for real. It was Poppy's happy place, her work haven, and she knew her close-knit staff supported her endeavor as a foster parent. If any of them made assumptions about her rocky romantic track record, they kept their opinions to themselves, unlike some of her friends, neighbors and former classmates, who seemed happy to offer unsolicited advice.

She waved to Annelise Wellington, Courtney's stepdaughter, who sat at a table in a somewhat private corner of the coffee shop. Poppy had told Annelise she'd be bringing Joey to their meeting and appreciated the other woman's discretion.

Courtney likely would have picked a table that put Poppy on display for all the world to see and judge. She shook off her insecurities as she approached the counter and ordered a caramel latte. She had to get over caring what other people thought. Part of being a foster parent would involve potentially helping older children navigate challenging situations where they might be subject to questions or criticisms from classmates.

Poppy didn't doubt her ability to offer unconditional love and support no matter the circumstance but also knew modeling self-confidence was more powerful than simply giving lip service to it.

Poppy recognized the manager on duty from her high school days. She might have even briefly dated Shane if Poppy remembered things correctly.

When the woman raised a questioning brow at the car seat, Poppy smiled and gestured her closer. "I'm sure you heard I'm fostering the baby left on my parents' porch at the beginning of the month." She kept her features neutral. "I'm so grateful the timing worked out so I could be a part of his life until we track down his mother and father." Her former classmate, whose name tag read Dawn, which Poppy hadn't remembered, offered a tight smile. "It's hard to tell if he looks like he belongs to one of the men in your family. Babies all look like grumpy old men when they're so young."

Poppy traced a finger over Joey's cheek while waiting for her order. "A little old man with the softest skin I've ever felt. No matter who he belongs to, I'm going to make sure this sweet boy ends up with a family who loves him."

Dawn stared at her for so long it became awkward. Finally, the barista at the coffee maker handed Poppy her drink.

"Well, nice talking to you." Poppy offered a smile then started to turn away.

"Wait." Dawn pulled a small plate from the stack on the counter behind her and used a pair of tongs to pull a blueberry muffin from the display case. She offered it to Poppy.

"I didn't order—"

"On the house," the woman said. "I'll carry it to your table since you've got your hands full."

"Thanks, but you don't have to do that." Poppy assumed that Dawn pitied her the way most of the town did. *Poor Poppy can't catch a man and has to resort to taking care of other people's children since she has none of her own.* "I feel lucky to have Joey in my life."

She thought about Leo and the way he'd slipped into her bed after Joey's final feeding last night and held her until she drifted off to sleep. "I'm happy."

Dawn walked around the edge of the counter. "You seem happy," she agreed, then glanced at Joey. "That baby is the lucky one. My husband, Jared, spent a few months in the foster care system when he was a toddler before being adopted by a couple down in Chatelaine. You're doing an admirable thing. Not many people are so selfless. A blueberry muffin is the least I can offer, but hopefully, it reminds you of what a difference you're making."

"Oh." Poppy's throat suddenly stung, and she swallowed back the emotion lodged there. "I appreciate you saying that."

"Everyone's talking about how amazing you are."

Poppy gave a quiet snort as she led the way to Annelise's table in the back. "I thought they were talking about the scandal Joey means for my family."

Dawn wrinkled her nose. "That, too. It's a small town. But they also admire you." She placed the muffin on the table. "*I* admire you."

"Thanks," Poppy repeated and set Joey's carrier in the infant carrier high chair Annelise had situated at the table as Dawn walked away.

"I don't know what that was about," Annelise said as Poppy slipped into the seat across from her after the woman walked off. "But I admire you, too. Not many people would step up for a baby like you have."

"Plenty of people are foster parents," Poppy countered. "I'm not special."

"I think you are," Annelise told her with a smile. "Other people do, too."

"I appreciate that." She tore off a bite of muffin and popped it in her mouth. The flavor was sweet, with the perfect amount of blueberry tanginess. "Honestly, I figured most people think I'm odd and possibly pathetic because I don't have a family of my own." She frowned then added, "Your stepmother certainly thinks so."

"I wouldn't put much stock in my *stepmonster's* opinion."

It made Poppy wonder if she'd been doing herself a disservice for longer than she realized. She assumed that her friends, family and people she knew in town considered her a failure at love and a bit of a bad luck charm when it came to relationships because that's how she'd seen herself. Had she simply been projecting her own fears onto other people?

Dawn didn't seem to believe that Poppy's desire to

be a foster parent and her dedication to Joey was anything other than altruistic. Of course, the baby situation hit close to home given that the new DNA results still hadn't been processed for her father, Micah and her uncle Hayden.

But Poppy couldn't control that. Whatever people thought about the mystery of Joey's parents, it didn't reflect on her. So what if she hadn't found love despite her many attempts at relationships? She led with her heart, which wasn't the worst offense in the world. Especially if she was her own harshest critic.

Poppy smiled at Annelise's nickname for Courtney. "Let's talk about your skincare line. I took the samples Courtney gave me to the spa. Everybody who tried them has been very impressed with the quality. How did you get started in this business?"

Annelise smiled, but it looked pained. "Let me start by saying I'm embarrassed if my stepmother pressured you into this meeting or anything. I'm proud of the line and would never want the FGR spa to feel obligated to carry any products. Your reputation is impeccable."

Poppy held up a hand. "And let *me* start by saying I was a bit put off initially. Courtney isn't exactly my favorite person."

Annelise's smile faded. "We have that in common, although the fact that she mentioned the line to you—"

"Oh, she did more than mention. She brought samples and talked you up quite a bit," Poppy explained. "To be honest, she seemed legitimately impressed by what you've created. She's a great hype person."

Annelise laughed softly. "I appreciate her support.

Maybe I've been wrong about Courtney and need to try harder to mend our relationship."

Poppy inclined her head in agreement. "I think a lot of Fortunes and Wellingtons have been wrong about each other over the years. It's never too late to try something new. But regardless of how I was introduced to your products, I would never carry anything or ask my staff to use or recommend products to clients that I don't believe in a hundred percent. As I told Courtney, most of the products we carry are from Texas-based companies. That's important to me and to the whole operation. The guest ranch sources as many items as possible from local or regional businesses. In fact, we just did a Valentine's Day special partnering with Abuela Rosa's chocolates. It was a big hit with the guests who came in for the weekend."

"I went to school with her granddaughter," Annelise murmured. "They are an amazing family, and those chocolates are to die for!"

"My staff would argue that your products are also to die for. If we can work something out, I think it would be great to carry AW GlowCare as part of our product line. Because you're local and a small operation, I'm hoping you might have some flexibility so that we could develop some products or packaging that will be unique for the spa. I love for our clients to be reminded of their experience at FGR once they get home."

She saw the moment Annelise forgot to be nervous or self-conscious about making a pitch. Her eyes lit up as she explained the origins of her interest in skincare and beauty products. Poppy loved the enthusiasm and appreciated that Annelise was dedicated but not overly boastful when discussing her talent and products.

As Annelise answered questions about the various aspects of the line's production, sourcing ingredients and her vision for the future, she became more animated, her earlier self-doubt forgotten.

"I love everything you've just told me." Poppy took the final bite of the muffin and savored not only the sweetness but also the reason Dawn had offered it to her in the first place. "I'd like you to meet a few of my staff members, particularly the aestheticians. Then we can discuss an initial order and potentially a long-term partnership."

"Really?" Annelise beamed. "It would be a dream come true to work with you and have AW GlowCare affiliated with the spa. Thank you, Poppy."

"It's a win-win," Poppy assured the other woman.

The family supported Rafe and Drake when they'd first come up with the Gift of Fortune initiative. Poppy had no reason—other than her own nagging doubt—to believe her brothers and cousins wouldn't support her in developing formal partnerships with local Emerald Ridge business owners.

She simply needed to take the risk to step out of her comfort zone. It was time she stopped hiding her light. If she didn't take risks or make her desires known, her dreams and goals would remain out of reach.

Joey, who'd been sleeping peacefully throughout the meeting, blinked awake and whimpered quietly.

"He's adorable," Annelise said as Poppy unstrapped the baby and lifted him from his carrier.

Poppy kissed the boy's forehead as she arranged him

in her arms. "It's only been a few weeks, but sometimes I can't remember my life before him." Or imagine her future without him and Leo, she added silently.

"Babies are easy to fall in love with."

"Very true," Poppy agreed, reaching for the premade bottle she'd packed in the diaper bag. "Don't feel like you have to keep us company. I'm going to feed him before heading out again."

Annelise checked her watch and then pushed back from the table. "I do need to get to a meeting with my chemists. They'll be so excited about this opportunity. Thanks again, Poppy."

"You should be thanking *me*," a shrill voice said from behind Poppy's shoulder. Joey startled. Poppy couldn't blame him, but she plastered a smile on her face as Courtney came to stand next to her.

"Hey, Courtney." Annelise's smile looked just as forced as Poppy's felt. "Yes, thank you for dropping off the samples, although you knew I had a plan for approaching Poppy."

The older woman waved away the comment. "You move too slow on opportunities, just like your father did. Sometimes a person has to take the proverbial bull by the horns to get what they want. Coming out on top is the end goal and the ends justify whatever means it takes to get there."

"Dad was a good man," Annelise said tightly. "His sense of honor never hurt his success, and he could feel proud at the end of the day about not only what he accomplished, but how he achieved his goals."

Courtney feigned a yawn. "Perhaps that was true for the men of your father's generation when life moved at a slower pace, especially out here in an insignificant cow town," the woman said.

Annelise had grown up in Emerald Ridge the same way Poppy had and seemed just as put off by her stepmother's assessment of the town and her late father. Poppy sat forward still cradling Joey, who was now happily taking down his bottle. "The FGR spa focuses on the history and legacy of the land my family owns. I think our customers will appreciate Annelise's products, not just because they're fabulous—which they are—but because of the ties she has to this community. Legacy is important."

Annelise shot her a grateful nod. "I'm honored by the opportunity. But now I really have to go. Courtney, lovely to see you as always. Poppy, I'm excited for a visit to the spa."

Poppy wasn't sure if Courtney had stopped by to insert herself into their meeting or if she wanted an opportunity to visit with her stepdaughter.

"I actually need to head to another meeting," Annelise said as she stood. She placed a hand on Courtney's arm. "Let's grab dinner later this week."

Courtney blinked several times, clearly shocked by the overture from her stepdaughter. "I'll have to check my calendar, but I could probably fit you in."

Poppy hid her grin as Annelise nodded. Mending her relationship with Courtney might be like trying to cuddle up to a porcupine, but at least Annelise was trying. She picked up her empty mug and Poppy's plate, then hurried to the front of the shop. Poppy would have liked to follow her out the front door. But she was stuck in place until Joey finished his feeding.

"I won't keep you," she said, hoping Courtney would take the hint. "I'm on the way to visit my mother when Joey's done." As soon as the words were out of her mouth, she regretted them. Courtney's gaze sharpened with interest.

"Is poor, sweet Shelley still hiding out at the hotel?"

Poppy tried not to growl. Thankfully Courtney didn't seem inclined to occupy Annelise's vacated chair. On the other hand, that would have made it more convenient for Poppy to *accidentally* kick her in the shin.

"I wouldn't call it hiding out. Everyone knows my mother's there."

"Yes, it's the talk of the town after your little situation." She waved a hand toward Joey.

"He's a baby, not a situation," Poppy clarified.

"Potato, potahto," Courtney chirped.

Poppy considered arguing, but that would only prolong this conversation, which she desperately wanted to end. "I'll tell her you said hello."

"Please do," Courtney cooed. "Send my apologies for not reaching out in her time of need." She heaved a dramatic sigh. "I understand what it's like to be a woman of a certain age on her own. Although, your mother is quite a few years older than me."

"She's also *not* alone," Poppy ground out.

"I'm just saying that it might be good to have a bit of space from your father at the moment. She'll have plenty of time to be there for you."

"My mother has always made time for me, my brothers and whoever needs her support."

"A regular *angel*," Courtney agreed. "Being so perfect all the time must get tiresome." She tsked quietly. "Or boring."

Poppy had never in her life wanted to inflict physical harm on another person, but Courtney brought out the worst in her, especially when she aimed her comments at Shelley.

Joey finished the bottle, and Poppy placed a burp cloth over her shoulder, lifted the boy and gently patted his back. "I have things to do, Courtney, and I'm certain you do as well. I appreciate you introducing me to Annelise's skincare line. She's extremely talented, and I look forward to working with her. If there's anything else you want to say, please just spit it out. I have too much going on right now to deal in games or puzzles."

Dawn, who'd been wiping down the table behind Courtney, leaned around the woman and gave Poppy a thumbs-up.

Maybe it wasn't so hard to stand up for herself and the people she loved after all. A couple of weeks with Joey had taught her so much about her life and what she wanted from it. One thing she wanted was to stop playing small.

Naturally, Courtney jumped at the chance to get more jabs in. "Well, I did hear you and Leo Leonetti made quite the dashing couple at the hotel ballroom on Valentine's Day…"

Poppy winced. Of course, people were talking. She reminded herself that other people's opinions about her were none of her business but deep down it still stung. "Did you want to ask where I got my dress because you heard it was so pretty or was there a specific question?"

"I tried to warn you about him."

Joey let out a burp, the most beautiful sound Poppy had heard in a long time because it meant she could pack the diaper bag, put the baby in his carrier and walk away.

"You warned me, and he took me to a nice dinner and dancing." She certainly hoped no one had heard about her cousin catching them in the far pasture. No way Micah would have gossiped about her.

"You should listen to me. Leo reminds me of Garth in a lot of ways. I've known men like your father. I *enjoy* men like your father. But I'm not at all certain Leo is the right man for a woman like you."

Courtney's suddenly silky tone made Poppy's skin crawl. The woman wouldn't dare make a play for her father, at least not during her parents' temporary separation. But what if things didn't work out? Would Courtney consider him fair game?

She scrambled to her feet, knocking over her empty coffee cup in the process.

"I need to go." She grabbed Joey's car seat and lifted him off the high chair.

Courtney grabbed her arm. "Your mom should be careful," she said in a hushed tone, as if sharing a secret. "I believe the text she received about your dad is true, and I think she does, too. I've also heard that some of the samples went missing. Garth is a powerful man and if he has a reason for those results to be delayed, you never know what he might do."

Ice clogged Poppy's veins. She yanked her arm free. "I know my dad. He wouldn't cheat on my mother or tamper with the DNA samples. He's a good man. Leo is, too, for that matter. He's a good friend to help me with Joey."

"It's sweet you think that, but be careful, Poppy. Leo is also a handsome man who likes women—*lots of women*, based on his reputation. You don't want to get hurt. Again."

No. This couldn't be happening. Poppy's concern for her own reputation and people talking about her felt ridiculously petty given Courtney's veiled accusation. How must her mother feel?

"I've got to go," she repeated, then rushed out of the coffee shop. She didn't bother returning to her parked car, too jittery to think about driving.

The hotel was only a couple blocks away, the February day unseasonably warm. She adjusted the cover on the infant carrier to protect Joey from direct sunlight as she hurried along the sidewalk.

By the time she knocked at her mother's room, sweat trickled between her shoulder blades, although she guessed nerves had more to do with it than the heat.

Shelley opened the door with a smile that quickly faded as she took in her appearance. "What happened, sweetie? What's wrong? How can I help?"

Poppy placed Joey's carrier on the coffee table in the small sitting room of the hotel suite. She busied herself with unstrapping and lifting him from the car seat. Otherwise, she might burst into tears if she met her mother's gaze. How was it possible that Shelley could be going through so much, yet her first concern remained her daughter's well-being?

Maybe she could take comfort in that. Even if her parents' marriage wasn't the model relationship she'd always thought, Shelley was still the perfect mother.

"Poppy?"

Cradling Joey to her chest, she sank onto the damask sofa. "Do you have water? It's warmer out than I expected." Her mother gave her a quizzical look but nodded and pulled a bottle from the minifridge under the walnut cabinet.

"Did you run all the way here?"

Poppy blinked, then realized her mom was making a joke and smiled. "I was at the coffee shop meeting with Annelise about her skincare line. Courtney showed up."

"What glad tidings did Courtney Wellington bring to you today?" Shelley lowered herself to the sofa next to Poppy. She seemed intent on looking anywhere but at Joey.

Poppy thought about lying to her mother, but she hated secrets. Hated the way the one involving the baby in her arms had the power to potentially tear apart her family.

"She said the text about Dad being Joey's father is probably true."

Shelley sucked in a harsh breath. "I didn't think anyone knew about that."

"Courtney said she heard it around town. That it's hard to keep secrets in Emerald Ridge."

"How ironic since no one seems to be able to unravel the mystery of Joey's mom and dad." Her mother leaned back against the sofa cushion and rolled her shoulders. "It doesn't matter. If it's true, everyone will eventually know."

"It might not be," Poppy insisted. "I refuse to believe Dad cheated on you." She waited for her mom to agree, but Shelley remained silent. "Mom, you know Dad loves you, right?"

"I do." Shelley sighed. "Like I told you before, sweetheart, it's not that simple."

"I'm worried about you," Poppy admitted thickly.

"I'll be okay." Shelley reached out a hand and tentatively placed it on Joey's back. The baby was sleeping peacefully, unaware of the tumultuous emotions surrounding him. Poppy took comfort in the soft sound of his breathing and the warmth of his little body against hers. "He's adorable and innocent."

"I love him so much, Mom." Poppy's voice cracked, and she squeezed her eyes shut.

"It's obvious. I felt the same way when you and your brothers were little. Babies are easy to fall in love with."

Just what Annelise told her. But so were men with dark eyes and a smile that made her knees go weak. Unfortunately, neither Joey nor Leo truly belonged to Poppy. But she wouldn't share those fears with her mother. She wanted to be the one to offer support, not take it.

"Would you like to hold him?" Poppy's heart tightened as she waited for her mother's answer. "Like you said, Joey is innocent in all of this."

Eventually, her mother nodded, hands trembling as she took the baby. Shelley's gaze softened when Joey made a soft gurgling noise and then burrowed his head in the crook of her neck.

"He's a snuggler," Poppy told her mom.

"I hope you know that the difficulties of this situation don't detract from my admiration for you. I'm glad Joey has you in his life." Shelley cradled the back of the baby's head with one hand and looked at Poppy. "Is it going to be difficult to eventually let him go?"

Poppy swallowed and dashed a tear from the corner of her eye. "Yes, but I knew that going in. Difficult things don't scare me anymore. I can deal with feeling my emotions even when they hurt."

"That's a gift, Poppy." Her mom reached out to hold her hand. "I hope it's one you never lose."

"You taught me." Poppy's voice cracked, but she continued, "You taught me how to love unconditionally, and I know that's how you love Dad. It's hard to see the two of you apart when you love each other so much."

Tears shimmered in her mother's soft blue eyes. "I'm trying to deal with the hard things, too."

"Why not together?" Poppy asked quietly.

"I do love your father." Shelley rested her chin on the top of Joey's head, something Poppy often did when she was holding him because his sweetness brought her a sense of comfort that nothing else offered. "But I let myself get lost in the role of wife and mother. That's on me, not him, but neither of us can deny the distance between us. Maybe we've become too comfortable in our marriage, but the situation with Joey made me see I don't want to settle anymore. I deserve a partner who treasures me, even if I'm not young, exciting or new."

"*Of course* you deserve that," Poppy agreed.

Shelley smiled, although it didn't reach her eyes. "You deserve that, too, sweetie. I might have taught you more than I meant to by devoting myself to your dad so fully. You need to know that you're special for who you are. Don't settle for anything less than a man who makes you feel that every day."

Poppy bit down on her lower lip to keep herself from saying that Leo made her feel special. He valued her and respected her. She'd seen for herself how much he'd changed over the years, but the fact remained that their relationship was based on a convenient arrangement. Convenient for both of them, perhaps, but he wanted it because being with her made his grandfather happy. Not necessarily because it made *him* happy.

"How are things with Leo?" Shelley asked as if she could read Poppy's mind.

"Temporary," Poppy answered before thinking better of it. Their date on Valentine's Day felt like a lifetime ago.

Shelley frowned. "Is that what you want?"

"It's all he's able to give." Her voice sounded sad and resigned even to her own ears.

"Not an answer to my question," her mother said. "Let me teach you something I'm learning only now, my sweet daughter. You are stronger than you know. Strong enough to put your needs and desires out there."

"Look at where that's gotten me in the past. Alone with a string of failed relationships littering the road behind me."

"It's gotten you to a place where those relationships ended because they weren't right. And now you're doing this beautiful, amazing thing for kids who need someone to love them. You have so much love to give. If Leo can't see that, he's a fool. If you make yourself smaller for him, well…"

"I'm the fool," Poppy whispered.

"And I didn't raise a fool." Shelley shifted Joey so she could place an arm around Poppy's shoulder.

Poppy leaned against her mother and took comfort in the warmth of the familiar embrace. It was time she did as her mom said and made her desires known. Maybe Leo would surprise her and be the man she needed him to. Perhaps Poppy would finally get that happily-ever-after she'd always wanted.

Chapter Twelve

"I thought it was just a burp, but there was projectile spit-up at the same time he had a blowout diaper. The kittens were prancing through the mess, and Humphrey looked as horrified as I felt."

Leo grinned as he watched his grandfather wipe tears of laughter from his eyes. He loved how much Enzo enjoyed the stories of Leo's escapades in parenting. *Not parenting*, he corrected silently.

Helping Poppy parent.

He was just the helper, not truly committed the way she was. Although if he was capable of commitment, it would be to Poppy and Joey. He'd always told himself he didn't want a serious relation and certainly not marriage. Never marriage. Except a lifetime with Poppy... well, any man would be lucky to have that.

"And you thought grapes could make a mess," Enzo said with another chuckle.

They sat at the farmhouse table in his mother's kitchen while she stood at the counter chopping vegetables for the minestrone soup she was making. Some of the color had returned to his grandfather's cheeks. Although Enzo still seemed to tire more quickly than before the setback,

Leo's mother reported that the doctor had been satisfied with his progress during his most recent checkup.

Leo glanced down at his phone, which had remained stubbornly silent for the entire duration of his visit. Poppy had left hours earlier for her meeting with Annelise Wellington, and Leo had expected her to let him know how things went when she returned to the house.

Not that she owed him a play-by-play on her daily movements, but they'd gotten into the habit of keeping each other informed under the guise of coordinating Joey's schedule.

The truth was he liked having somebody to check in with. More importantly, he liked *Poppy* being that somebody.

Enzo finished his last bite of the tomato-and-hummus sandwich Martina had served for lunch and pushed back from the table. Leo also stood and picked up his grandfather's empty plate before Enzo could.

"I'll clean up for you, Papa," Leo offered. The old man had taken the last few bites around a series of yawns. "Why don't you head to your room for a rest?"

"I'm not an invalid," he grumbled. "I can put my own plate in the dishwasher."

Before Leo could answer, his mother snorted. "Everyone knows you're capable of clearing your plate, but you should never reject an offer of help, especially from my beloved son. Leo has been an expert at avoiding the dishwasher until recently—one more thing to credit to Poppy, I presume." His mother raised a brow.

It was Leo's turn to grumble. "I knew how to load an empty dishwasher before Poppy."

"Knowing and doing are two different things," his mother retorted, making Enzo smile again.

"I'm proud of you, Leo," his grandfather said.

While the words should have made Leo happy, his gut twisted. He appreciated his grandfather's pride but felt undeserving of it in some deep part of his soul. Especially given that his whole motivation for helping with Poppy had been contrived to do exactly that.

"I think I will take a little rest after all," Enzo said as he shuffled toward the back staircase that led to the second-floor bedrooms from the kitchen. "Bring Poppy and the baby to see me again. Little Joey makes me feel younger than I am, and that's always a good thing."

"I will, Papa, very soon. I should get back to the office," he told his mother after loading the dishwasher. "Unless you need help here?"

"No, I've got it handled." She wiped her hands on a dish towel and patted his cheek the way she used to when he was a kid. "But can you stay and talk for a minute?"

"Sure, Mom, what's up? Is it about the new label redesign? Gia said you had some thoughts on that."

"It's about you and Poppy Fortune."

Leo tried not to react, but something serious in his mother's gaze made him wary.

"I promise I'm even more helpful at her place, and we had a great time on Valentine's Day. Thank you again for watching Joey. You were right, as always. She deserves to be treated like a queen."

"And that's what you're doing?" He heard the doubt in his mother's tone, which grated at his pride.

"I hope so."

"She's special," his mother said, as if that would explain the reason for this conversation, one he definitely hadn't bargained for.

He held his hands up high and wiggled them. "Preaching to the choir." His mother didn't laugh at the lame joke.

"What are your intentions when it comes to Poppy Fortune?"

Leo tried not to cringe at the bluntness of the question and the fact that he didn't know how to answer it. "Isn't that something her parents should be asking?"

Once again, his mother didn't smile at his attempt at humor. "Her parents are dealing with a lot. Otherwise, I'm sure they would have asked you that question long before now. But *I'm* asking it now. Your previous relationship with her was short lived, but I know she meant something to you. This is a second chance if you're smart enough to take it, Leo."

She reached for his arm, but he stepped away, in no mood to pretend this wasn't a gently worded interrogation.

"My intention is to help her with the baby. Don't you think I'm doing a good job of it?"

"I've seen you with Joey." His mother smiled almost wistfully. "It's obvious you care about him, and I know you, Leo. You're fantastic at meeting a goal when you set your mind to it. But I'm not talking about your mind right now. I'm talking about your heart *and* Poppy's heart."

"Poppy loves Joey," he said, as if she needed him to defend her.

"Yes." Martina nodded. "I think it's quite possible that she also loves you."

His heart felt like it was seizing in his chest. The words were thrilling and terrifying in equal measure.

"We're friends, Mom. We agreed on that."

"You're a lot of things, Leo. You are smart, passionate and committed to this family. I appreciate all of those. But I never took you to be a coward."

"Ouch."

"You need to hear this," his mother insisted. "If you can't be the man Poppy needs, and not just when it comes to Joey, but as a true partner, you have to let her go."

He felt his head snap back like his mother had slapped him. And he couldn't even be angry with her because he deserved her doubt. He didn't want to hurt Poppy, but he also wasn't ready to let her go. Nowhere near ready.

"Come on, Mom. It isn't as if I kidnapped her. We both understand the arrangement."

Martina's lips rolled together as if she was holding back for his benefit. Finally, she blew out a breath. "It isn't as simple as you're making it out to be. Emotions are complicated—*people* are complicated. When a woman opens her heart and lets a man in, he has a responsibility to either meet her halfway or admit that he can't. Pretending only leads to heartbreak for everyone, whether or not your intentions are honorable."

His mother's grip tightened on the dish towel, her knuckles as white as tiny snowballs.

"Mom, is this about Poppy and me, or are you talking about Dad? You know he loved you."

"I'm not speaking ill of your father. He was a good man. He did the best he could with a life he didn't necessarily want."

"What do you mean? Of course Dad wanted this life.

He wanted you." He hated the way his stomach twisted in response to her words. Hated that despite his denial, a part of him knew it was true.

"He wanted freedom. He wanted to travel and see the world, just like you did before he died and you took over."

"I had plenty of time to travel after college," he argued. "I always understood I'd come back. I'm fine with it. What does any of this have to do with Poppy?"

"I know you care about her, but sometimes that isn't enough. Don't commit to something to make your grandfather happy. It isn't fair to you or her."

"She's Joey's foster parent. It's temporary, just like…"

His mother sighed. "Just like your relationship. I know what I see when I look at her. When she looks at the baby and you, how things started might have been temporary, but it could be more if you want it to."

Did he want that? Leo's heart began to beat an unsteady rhythm. Sure, he'd considered what might happen between him and Poppy, but having his mother question him felt different. It felt real, and he wasn't sure he could deal with it. But could he let her and Joey go at this point? He'd messed up his chance with her five years earlier and the regret had never fully faded. Now he was so much more invested and it terrified him.

"Am I like Dad?" he asked, unsure whether he wanted to hear the answer. "I know I look like him, but is it more than that?"

"There are parts of you that remind me of your father, just like there are ways your sisters take after him. He had a gift with the grapes and your leadership capabilities. Antonia's financial acumen." She smiled and shook her head. "Gia embodies his way of charming the customers. Franco had everything, but he didn't appreciate this life. It wasn't the one that filled his soul."

"I'm sorry, Mom," he said, but she waved away his apology.

"We muddled through, and there were aspects of our life together that he loved desperately. Being a father was on that list. I can't tell you what you want, Leo, but whatever it is, I want you to have it. Of course, it would make me happy if you chose Poppy, but I also understand if you don't want all the responsibility that comes with her. I think she will as well, but you can't pretend."

Leo's chest burned with longing, but he couldn't name what he yearned for.

"If this place starts to make you feel confined, we'll find a way to give you space and freedom."

Never before had anyone acknowledged that he'd taken on the mantle of CEO without being given the chance to decide if that was the role he truly wanted.

His mother seemed to take his lack of an answer as a sign. "Is that what you want?" she asked. "More freedom?"

"I'm involved with a woman whose life is the opposite of what I thought I wanted," he admitted, more to himself than his mother. Then he looked at her. "I don't want to hurt her."

"I know, son, but if you act like someone you're not to make other people happy, then you're the one who's going to be hurt. I don't want that."

His phone trilled, breaking the tense heaviness of emotion that hung in the air with a series of rapid-fire chimes. "Must be something important," Martina said as he moved toward the kitchen table where he'd left it.

He muttered a curse and then glanced up at his mom. "Joey's sick." He pocketed the phone, already heading toward the door.

Her eyes widening in concern, his mother took a step toward him. "What's wrong?"

"I'm not sure," he replied. "Poppy texted that he seemed drowsy this morning and lethargic when she left her mom's, but he'd spiked a fever by the time she got home. She called the pediatrician, and they told her to head to the ER. I'm meeting her there."

Martina pressed a hand to her heart. "Babies get sick, Leo," she said reassuringly. "The doctors will take care of him. He'll be fine."

"Of course, he will," Leo agreed. "I'll call you later, Mom."

He dashed from the house to his truck, and gravel spit up behind him as he peeled out of the driveway. Joey would be fine. He had to be because Leo couldn't imagine his life if something happened to the boy.

Poppy disconnected the call and leaned back against the uncomfortable chair in the small pediatric unit at the county hospital. She could see the doorway to Joey's room from where she sat. He was being monitored so if anything happened while she was out of the room, she'd know.

Her mother had offered to drive over and keep Poppy company, but it was already nearly nine at night, so there'd be no point. As soon as Leo returned from gathering a few things for her overnight stay with Joey, Poppy would climb into the reclining chair next to his bassinet and settle in for what promised to be a restless few hours of sleep.

Her phone pinged with messages from both her brothers and her dad, sending good thoughts for the baby. She closed her eyes and willed herself not to cry. Tears wouldn't do any good, and Joey's fever had finally broken an hour earlier, so the on-call pediatrician hoped he'd be discharged in the morning.

It was difficult to believe how much had changed from a couple weeks earlier when she'd spent the night at this same hospital waiting to take Joey home. At that point, she'd felt sympathy for the abandoned baby and a call to help care for him.

Now she loved the boy with her whole heart.

And speaking of love…she watched Leo exit the elevator and walk down the hall toward her. There'd been no hesitation in her decision to text him first after talking to the pediatrician, and he'd been waiting at the entrance of the ER when she arrived with Joey.

Leo Leonetti continued to blow her away with the way he'd gone all in with her and Joey. It still felt somewhat baffling that a man who professed to be almost allergic to relationships so easily gave her what she needed, both in his support of Joey and the way he made Poppy feel.

She didn't think that kind of dedication could be faked, and although he hadn't spoken the words aloud, she couldn't help but believe his stance on commitment and romantic love might be changing. Their time together had certainly transformed Poppy, or at least made her rethink her views on dating.

Yes, she'd had some failures when it came to men, but she realized now she still believed in love. She wanted love, even with the scandal surrounding her family and learning that her parents' relationship wasn't perfect.

She had been working from an ideal in her mind that maybe no one could live up to, even herself. Leo might not say the words, but his actions, the way he looked at her, held and touched her body—all of those spoke to their growing bond.

But Poppy also understood after the conversation with her mother that she wanted the words, too. Not flowery sonnets or grand gestures, but she wanted to know that the man she cared about loved her.

She deserved someone who would put her first, not just let her do the heavy lifting. She knew Leo could be that man, even if he didn't realize it yet. The conversation with her mother had been a light-bulb moment for Poppy, pushing her out of her comfort zone and into admitting she *did* want more. Maybe Leo needed the same thing.

She stood as he entered the room. He didn't hesitate to wrap his arms around her after he deposited her bag on the carpeted floor. Who was she kidding?

Poppy had already fallen hard and fast. She wanted a real romance with Leo, at least once they were certain Joey would be okay.

But at the moment, she couldn't focus on any future other than Joey's and the baby getting better.

"It's going to be okay," Leo said, able to read her thoughts again. "His fever's gone, and he's getting good care."

She let out a little sob, her worry coalescing into tears after holding them back for the baby's sake. "I know, and I'm so grateful for the doctors and nurses. But why,

Leo? Why did he get that fever? We don't have an answer, and what if it's my fault?"

"It's not your fault," he assured her in that deep, rumbly tone.

She pulled back to look into his deep brown eyes, searching them for some inkling of the doubt swirling through her.

"You don't know that. I had him out in that coffee shop, and who knows what kind of germs other customers were breathing on him? Maybe the guy we shared an elevator with at the hotel had some kind of virus—"

"Sometimes babies get sick."

"But why did *my* baby get sick?" she demanded like Leo could give her a satisfying answer.

"*Our* baby," he responded, with an emphasis that made her heart lurch, "is going to be okay. You noticed it right away and called the doctor. You took care of him."

"I hated that night he spent in the hospital after being left on my parents' porch, and I hate this even more."

"But you're here with him." He smoothed her hair away from her face. "And you have me if you want."

"They said only one person could stay in the room."

He didn't miss a beat in offering, "I'll sleep on one of these chairs. If you want me to stay, I will."

It was tempting to accept the offer. Even before Leo had started spending every night in her bed, the fact that he was asleep down the hall gave her so much comfort.

"But what about tomorrow? One of us needs to be awake. Plus, Humphrey and the kittens will be nervous without me there. You don't mind staying at my house on your own?"

"Of course I'll stay," he replied gruffly.

He hugged her again, and they stood together for several minutes in companionable silence. Poppy didn't need him to speak. As she was coming to rely on, his actions told her everything she needed to know.

Leo held her hand as they returned to Joey's room, and while she washed her face and brushed her teeth in the connecting bathroom, he conferred with the nurse, then fed Joey and changed his diaper. Ready for bed, Poppy ran a hand over the boy's forehead, which remained blessedly cool.

The nurse checked the output in his diaper, and instead of returning him to the bassinet, Leo sat on the chair next to the bassinet as if he wasn't ready to let the baby go.

Poppy's heart felt like it was bursting with a myriad of emotions. This incident reminded her about the uncertainty of life and how important it was not to let fear stop her from living the way she wanted.

After Leo gently tucked Joey and her into their respective beds, Poppy watched the door close behind him, staring at the acoustic tiles on the hospital room ceiling for a long time before drifting off to sleep.

Leo cared for her. Deeply. She knew it in her gut.

Once things were back to normal with Joey, she would tell him her feelings and hopefully give him the confidence to acknowledge his. No matter what happened with the DNA tests and how long she got to keep Joey, his presence in her life would always be a blessing because it had taught her that some things were truly worth fighting for.

Chapter Thirteen

As Leo opened the door to Poppy's house the following evening, he was greeted by an incredible smell, along with music from the kitchen.

He turned the corner from the entryway to see Poppy dancing around the island with Joey in her arms. The day had been a rough one with production delays and frustrated retail outlets. Plus, there was the constant worry in the back of his mind about how the baby was doing, even though she sent him some pics of Joey cooing and kicking on his activity blanket. The baby seemed to have made a quick and complete recovery from his scary fever the previous night, but Leo had trouble shaking his anxiety.

His dad had seemed fine when he said goodbye to him before that last trip to Italy, and he'd been dead two days after Leo landed. His grandfather had been agitated at their dinner, but not alarmingly so, and then he'd wound up in the hospital. This was part of the reason Leo didn't trust himself to focus on other areas of his life besides work. He could leave stressful tasks at the office overnight. No matter how bad things were, they'd still be waiting the following morning.

People, however, weren't the same. They could get hurt—or die—and there was nothing he could do about it if he wasn't there to protect them, and maybe not even then.

Loving people simply wasn't safe, and his heart expanded in his chest watching Poppy twirl the baby. She had no rhythm, making her staccato dance moves even more charming.

Leo couldn't continue to ignore how he felt about her, not when they were together playing house and family each night. The way to save himself from being hurt again was to keep his heart out of the mix. As much as it killed him to admit it, doing that meant not letting himself fall in love with her.

He just hoped it wasn't already too late…

Poppy gave a startled cry that quickly turned into laughter as she noticed him standing in the doorway.

"Care to join us?" She held out a hand. It was all he could do to keep himself from reaching for her, to refrain from dropping to his knees and begging her never to leave. Never to put herself at any risk…never to break his heart.

But that was a promise no one could make. He gave a slight shake of his head. "I left my dancing shoes at the office."

She scrunched up her nose. "You're just trying to avoid me tromping all over your feet again."

He wanted to avoid a lot of things, and what a stupid coward he was for all of it.

She gave the Bluetooth speaker the command to turn off, then approached him. "How about a quieter greeting?" She leaned in to kiss him.

He wanted to freeze this moment and memorize everything about it. The warmth of her, this kitchen and the way he felt at home every time he walked into it.

Poppy's beautiful green eyes, the color of the soft shoots of the first leaves growing on the grapevines. The way she always smelled like sunshine. Even on a dark February night. The baby nestled in her arms and the way he'd captured Leo's heart from the first time he'd held him...

"It smells delicious," he said, grasping for some neutral subject to help him find purchase when it felt like he was free-falling off an emotional cliff. "I was planning on takeout. I thought you'd be exhausted after last night."

Poppy grinned, her eyes sparkling. "Actually, I feel energized with relief that Joey is himself again. That fever freaked me out, you know?"

He nodded and took a step away from her. "Still, you didn't have to make dinner." It was a stupid thing to say. Poppy made supper most nights when she was at the house, just like he did if he was taking a turn with the baby in the afternoon.

It doesn't mean anything, he reminded himself. *It's food. People have to eat, typically three times a day.*

She handed Joey to him, and Leo tried not to notice the baby's familiar weight, warmth or the milky smell that radiated from him along with the scent of lavender.

Poppy must have bathed him, which always made the boy kick and coo delightedly. Leo loved bath time. He was going to miss bath time. If someone would have suggested a few years ago that such a simple task would mean so much to him, he would have laughed in their face. He'd been so sure he wasn't built for anything other than his work and having fun. No-strings-attached fun. But maybe there was more to him than he thought and he could be that man for Poppy and Joey.

She grabbed two potholders sitting on the counter and opened the oven door.

"It's three-cheese baked manicotti," she said. "Your mom called earlier to check on Joey, and I asked her about your favorite meal. She gave me the recipe along with instructions for making tiramisu."

Beads of sweat popped out on Leo's forehead. "You made tiramisu?"

She placed the red casserole dish on top of the stove and shrugged, her smile still wide and trusting. "I thought we could both use a home-cooked meal, and I wanted to do something for you."

He shook his head but didn't move, rooted in place. "You don't owe me anything, Poppy."

"You've been so supportive and helpful. I couldn't have managed this without you, Leo. I wouldn't have wanted to either. This is my way of thanking you for it."

"We have an arrangement." His voice sounded hollow. "I'm helping you because it makes me look good to my grandfather. It makes him happy."

She inclined her head. "Enzo is the best. I love watching him with Joey but impressing him was how this started. It's become more now, hasn't it?"

He forced himself not to smile even though it killed him. "Sure," he relented. "We're friends. We'll continue to be friends."

A crease appeared between her brows. "You have to know it's more than that for me, Leo. I—"

"Don't say it, Poppy. You can't say it. We had an arrangement. Eventually, those DNA tests will come back, and you'll know the identity of Joey's father. From there, you can track down his mother and this—" he waved a hand in the general direction of her house "—will be over."

She stared at him for a long moment and said, "This is my life. My home. It's not going to be over, and I don't want it to."

"You know what I mean."

"I do," she agreed. A chill entered her tone, a cold completely at odds with the warmth she'd exuded moments earlier. His fault. *Always* his fault.

"We're friends," he repeated. "Nothing has to change if we don't make it."

"I love you," she said simply.

The words hung between them like dandelion fluff floating on the air in the heat of summer.

"You love the idea of us," he answered. "Caring for a newborn was overwhelming at first, and I relieved some of that pressure. But it's different now. You don't need me."

She walked toward him, her features stripped of emotion. The only tell that revealed the control she struggled with was her fists clenched at her sides.

"Don't mansplain my feelings to me, Leo. That's low, even for you."

He didn't argue with her accusation because he felt so low it was like his stomach scraped the floor.

"I'm sorry, Poppy."

"For what?" she demanded, lifting Joey from his arms like he no longer had a right to hold the baby. No, she wouldn't do that. They had an agreement. They were a team.

"I'm not the one changing things." He ran a hand through his hair, grasping for a way to make her understand. "I can't be the white-picket-fence partner you want."

"I don't *want* a fence," she shot back.

"You know what I mean." He blew out a frustrated breath. How had things gone to hell so quickly?

"I want *you*."

Damn it. Why did she have to keep going? Was she trying to wreck them both?

"Please, Poppy." He crossed his arms over his chest to keep from reaching for her. "Things are fine the way they are. If you could just—"

"Fine isn't good enough." She rubbed a hand over Joey's back when the boy began to fuss, likely attuned to the tension between the only caregivers he knew. "I told you I love you. I'm not lowering my expectations or what I want from our relationship because you can't handle it."

"We had an *arrangement*," he repeated through clenched teeth, willing her to understand what this was doing to him. To both of them. "Love wasn't part of it."

"I can't tell whether you're lying on purpose or you really believe the lines you're trying to feed me." She backed away, and he wanted to shout in protest. "It doesn't matter. I'm not settling. This isn't me asking for too much—it's about what you can't give. You've been a huge help, and I appreciate that. I'm glad your grandfather has enjoyed watching you in this role with Joey. You're a natural, Leo."

She spoke the words sincerely and he wanted to be grateful, but the compliment lodged between his ribs like a knife. "Why do I feel like there's a *but* coming?"

She shrugged. "But you missed your calling as an actor because you sure had me fooled. I thought you cared about me and not just because of the baby."

"I *do* care."

"Not in the way I need you to."

He didn't argue. What could he say? That she deserved better...more than he could give. Weren't his track record and his father's unhappiness proof of that?

"You should go." Those three words felt like a round of bullets to his heart.

"It doesn't have to be this way."

"What other way would you have it?" She posed the question like she was asking about the weather. Leo scrambled for an answer, but he had nothing to offer. Nothing that would make her feel better or ease the pain piercing his gut.

He took a step toward the hallway leading to the bedrooms, but Poppy held up a hand.

"I need you to go now. I'll pack your stuff, and you can pick it up from the porch tomorrow morning. Thank you again for your help. I wasn't lying when I said I couldn't have done this without you."

Her green eyes were sad when they met his. "I wasn't lying about any of it."

Something about the sentence felt unfinished, as if insinuating that *he* was the liar. And maybe he had been lying to both of them, acting as if he could handle more. Pretending he could be the man she said she saw in him. The one his grandpa so desperately wanted him to be.

He should fight or argue. A bigger man would. A better man.

Leo only turned and walked out of the house into the dark, cold night, feeling more alone than he ever had. He understood, even if Poppy didn't, that she could have done everything without him. He hadn't been the hero to step in and rescue her.

She was plenty capable of that on her own, and she'd done her best to save him. But a person could only be saved if they wanted to. Although anyone would tell him his logic was twisted, it seemed safer to remain in the solitary confinement he'd sentenced his heart to. Because as much as that treacherous organ ached as he drove away, he knew the risk of opening it fully would be so much worse.

"I know it sucks for you, Pop-Tart, but I have to say, this is the best meal I've had in a long time. I should text Leo Leonetti and thank him for being a doofus."

Poppy offered Rafe a weak smile across the table. The baked manicotti she'd made had gone cold on the stove while she sat with Joey in her arms and cried her eyes out after Leo left.

Her tears weren't because she'd been a fool to let Leo in, the way she'd felt after almost every one of her other breakups. This time, she didn't regret loving Leo. The only way to claim the future she wanted was to keep her heart open, no matter how many times it got crushed in the process.

Somehow, she couldn't imagine getting over this one. Yet, her tears had been as much for Leo as for herself. He loved her. Despite all the stupid things he'd said and the ways he'd denied his feelings, she *knew* he loved her.

How sad was it that he was too scared to admit it? Too committed to staying safe that he couldn't take what she offered and reciprocate those emotions.

Rafe had texted her about a half hour after Leo walked out. On his way home, he'd seen the truck speeding away from the ranch and had been concerned about another potential issue with Joey.

Poppy'd started to return her brother's message with a vague everything is fine text of her own.

But no. Part of being true to herself was acknowledging the good with the bad and asking for support. Being willing to accept it instead of feeling like her role—the only way she could add value—was offering it to the people in her life.

So she'd dashed off the truth to her brother.

I told him I loved him. He drove away like the devil was chasing him.

Rafe's response had been immediate.

I'll be there in five.

She had just enough time to splash cold water on her face and dry her cheeks before her brother burst through the front door.

He'd been spitting mad and admitted he'd been unsure whether to start at her house or chase after Leo and knock his lights out.

"No lights knocking," Poppy'd told him, then instructed him to reheat portions of the manicotti while she put Joey down for bed.

She was happy Rafe enjoyed the meal because her first bite tasted like sawdust in her mouth.

She sipped on a glass of wine, a pinot grigio Leo had brought over at some point, special from his private collection. She'd expected to share the bottle with him, but they wouldn't be sharing anything.

Not anymore.

"Maybe I came on too strong," she murmured, even though she didn't believe it.

One of her brother's thick brows rose. "You're perfect, sis, and I'm sure however you treated Leo was also perfect."

"You're right. It wasn't too strong. The truth is, I didn't come on to him at all. I just fell in love."

"Oh, Pop Rocks." Rafe sighed like he was disappointed but not surprised.

"He loves me, too," she said because that's what she believed to her core.

"Then what's the problem?"

"Men are dumb."

Her brother laughed as he stabbed a piece of pasta. "I won't argue that point. It seemed like Leo was having a good time with you and Joey. Any man who willingly changes diapers and scoops cat litter is either a masochist or in love."

He paused with the fork almost to his mouth. "They might be one and the same."

She dipped her fork into the sauce and tasted it. "This is good."

"Delicious," Rafe confirmed. "You said it's Leo's favorite?"

"According to his mom."

"Then he must have been extra spooked to walk away before eating."

Poppy rolled her eyes. "I didn't give him a choice. I kicked him out."

Rafe stopped chewing and stared at her. "*You* ended it?"

"Yes. Why do you sound shocked? I told him I loved him, and he told me not to."

"Rough." Rafe cringed then placed his fork on the table. "I'm surprised because you typically hang on until the bitter end. Good for you. It's about time you started owning what a catch you are. I didn't think Leo was as big of an idiot as some of the other guys you've dated, but maybe I was wrong."

"My previous boyfriends weren't idiots."

Rafe definitely thought they had been by the look on his face. A wistful smile played in the corners of his mouth. "Bridget used to get so mad at how you'd let them walk all over you."

Poppy's face burned, but so did her heart. Rafe very rarely spoke about the wife and daughter he lost in that accident.

"I should have listened to her. Although you could argue that Leo and I never officially dated, so maybe he can't be considered a boyfriend."

"He helped to raise a baby, lived with you, took you out for the big V Day. I assume there were benefits between friends?"

"Oh, my gosh, we can't talk about *benefits*. You are my brother."

"I guess you don't need to answer because your voice

is reaching decibels I didn't even know were possible for a human to hear. That tells me everything."

She pushed back from the table and picked up their bowls to take them to the sink. "Enough about the pathetic state of my life. Tell me something about you."

"Not much to tell." Rafe crossed the kitchen and leaned one hip against the counter. "I've been working on the Gift of Fortune program, but things are stalled because one of the recipients is ghosting me."

"Not interested?" Poppy asked, hiding her smile. Rafe wasn't used to being ignored.

"Hard to tell since she won't return my calls." He shrugged. "I don't get it. The woman, Heidi, is a single mom with twins. She has to need a break."

Poppy laughed. "I'm taking care of one baby so I can only imagine the effort two takes on your own."

"Right. So why won't she respond to the invitation? It's a free week at the ranch."

The frustration in his tone chased away her smile. This was important to her brother, and she admired what he was trying to do with the generous program.

"You never know what's going on in another person's life, Rafe."

"Tell me about it," he muttered.

"But it's amazing that you're working so hard to bring happiness to people who might not find it on their own. Give it some time."

"Thanks, Pop." Rafe blew out a breath then gently grabbed her arm and circled her wrist with his big hand. "You deserve to be happy, too."

"That makes two of us," she told him quietly. His lips thinned as he released her to stand.

Her brother processed grief in his solitary way, but she didn't like to see anyone in her family sad. Rafe hadn't been happy for a long time.

"You want a piece of tiramisu for the road?" she asked. "I'm going to take some to Dad tomorrow."

"I want a bigger piece than you give him. I might take a selfie of me eating it and send it to Leo with the one-finger salute."

Poppy sighed then smiled, as her brother expected her to. Her family members were experts at changing the subject and lightening the mood. "Do you think Dad could be Joey's father?"

She took the glass dish of tiramisu out of the refrigerator, then grabbed plastic to-go containers from under the island, her brother silent at that question.

"I want to say no and believe it. Dad is very convincing in his denials."

"But how do we explain the text? That's pretty damning."

Rafe shrugged. "Sure, but if a person was so determined for the truth to come out, why would they send the message anonymously?"

Poppy loaded a generous square of the dessert into a to-go container, then placed the lid on it, licking a bit of cream off her thumb. "Good point. Mom says the separation isn't just about Joey. It's hard to fathom that when they always seemed to get along."

Rafe placed his hands over hers. "Maybe that's the lesson. Things might seem okay on the surface, but that doesn't mean they are."

She hugged her brother. "One of these days, everything will be okay again."

Rafe nodded. "You'll be okay, Pop."

She locked the door behind him, and Poppy leaned her back against it. The tears had dried, but her heart felt empty and hollow.

Humphrey climbed off the couch and with a soft whine, trotted over to her, head butting her thigh. "I miss him, too," she told the dog, "but the good news for you is that the empty space in my bed is available again."

His tail wagged as if he understood her words. Poppy walked to her bedroom, brokenhearted but proud of herself for staying true to the woman she wanted to be. If Leo Leonetti couldn't give it to her, she'd find it on her own. Maybe that was the lesson all along.

Chapter Fourteen

The next morning, Poppy's emptiness had shifted into a fiery ball of anger. She was trying her best to be brave, take risks and not worry about what other people thought as long as she followed her heart. Yet she was surrounded by people, men in particular, who refused to show that kind of courage.

She might not be happy that her mother had moved out but admired Shelley's willingness to ignore potential gossip and be true to herself.

Leo wasn't doing that. She no longer knew if the man she'd fallen in love with over these weeks together was the true Leo. Did fear prevent him from becoming the man she saw when she looked at him?

Or maybe she had it backward, and he truly didn't want a commitment but was too afraid to admit that and disappoint his grandfather.

Then there was her oldest brother, who'd loved with all of his heart but wore his grief at the tragic loss he'd suffered like a badge of honor. Poppy knew his late wife wouldn't have wanted that for him. Bridget would have given him a kick in the butt to get back on that horse and open his heart again.

Poppy hoped he eventually met a woman who could convince him to do that.

And as for her father…

She entered her childhood home without bothering to knock and let the door slam shut behind her.

"I'm in the study," Garth called out.

Poppy practically stomped down the hallway to the wood-paneled room, her father's inner sanctum. As a kid, she'd sneak into the library to sit at the chair behind his desk. She and her brothers weren't allowed to play in this room, but Poppy hadn't been playing. Even as an eight-year-old girl, she'd been thinking about family and the future.

She knew what she wanted, and while a few failed relationships had forced her off course, she was back and not in the mood to listen to any more excuses, rationalizations— or God forbid—gaslighting.

"Hello, my beautiful girl," her father said, studying her over the top of his tortoiseshell readers. "What's all that?"

In addition to Joey's car seat slung over one arm, Poppy held a plate of manicotti and half the leftover tiramisu. The rest would go to the staff lounge at the spa, but her father had a big sweet tooth. Poppy might be angry, but she still loved the guy.

"I brought you leftovers. I'll put them in the fridge in a minute." Poppy placed Joey's infant carrier on the round work table that sat in one corner.

"A visit from my best girl and homemade lunch." Garth raised his hands in the air. "Am I a lucky man or what?"

Poppy stared at him for several long seconds, waiting for him to recant that bit of tomfoolery. When he didn't, she shook her head in exasperation. "Seriously, Dad? Right now, we are going with door number two, which is *or what*."

He blinked at her, clearly shocked at being called out on his pretend joviality. His face crumpled, shoulders slumping as he took off the reading glasses and placed them on the desk.

"Before this month, that statement would have been true. I've always been lucky." He stared at the black blotter covering the walnut wood like he was studying tea leaves. "Lucky to live on this ranch with your mother. Lucky to have three amazing kids. I don't know how it all went so wrong so fast."

Poppy stepped closer. "Do you mean that? Do you truly have no idea what happened between you and Mom?"

Her father's head snapped up, and he jabbed a finger in the direction of the carrier. "I know for damn sure I'm not that boy's father."

At the sound of shouting, Joey let out a weak cry. Poppy flashed her father a quelling glare, then went to unstrap the boy and lifted him into her arms.

"He isn't the only reason she left."

"She hadn't packed her bags before then."

Poppy came forward and lowered herself into one of the leather chairs in front of her father's desk. She'd been allowed into his lair upon invitation as a kid and had loved sitting across from him doing her homework while he managed the guest ranch from the same seat his father had. The same chair where her great-grandfather before him had sat. So much history in this house, and yet some of the things that needed to be said were kept silent.

"Mom says the two of you have been having problems for a while."

Garth frowned like the words were hard to acknowledge but eventually nodded.

"I didn't cheat on her," he repeated in a solemn tone.

It might be naivety or wishful thinking, but Poppy believed him.

"Then how did it get to this point, and why aren't you fighting for her?"

Her questions registered slowly on her father's face, a slight pull at the corners of his mouth and a flash of uncertainty in his dark eyes. "I'm not sure I know how on either count," he admitted finally.

"Dad."

"It's true. Your mom and I have had an easy go of it. Sure, we've dealt with issues over the years. Everyone does, but…" He pulled at his thick salt-and-pepper hair with one hand. "It's embarrassing to admit, especially to my daughter, but I've let her do the heavy lifting on the relationship side. Your mom is the glue that keeps this family and our marriage together."

Poppy swallowed back the emotion that swelled in her throat. "She's the glue, but she has needs, too, Dad."

"I appreciate that." He shook his head. "I'm just not sure I know how to meet them."

How odd to be in the position of offering relationship advice to her father, a turn of events neither of them likely had expected.

Yet, in some ways, this was another example of Poppy stepping out of her comfort zone to be brave. She wanted to make a difference, not only in the world but in the lives of her family. That couldn't happen if she didn't speak up. Secrets and assumptions wouldn't help anyone.

"You might be terrible at it," she told her father, earning a disbelieving snort. "But you won't know if you don't try, Dad. If I've learned anything from taking care of Joey this month and the way things turned out with Leo, it's that being willing to fail is the only path to success. It makes the journey that much sweeter. If you love Mom, you've got to try to find a way to make her believe it again. Not just for your sake but for hers. Trust me when I tell you that relationships are way more satisfying when both people put in the effort."

"Is that what you and Leo have?"

Poppy breathed out a sigh of relief, realizing her brother hadn't left her house and immediately shared her latest failure with the rest of the family.

She shook her head. "I thought so, but he didn't feel the same, so I ended things."

"Oh, honey, I'm sorry. The right guy is out there for you. I know that."

Her heart still rebelled against the idea that Leo wasn't that man, but she nodded. "I don't have regrets, Dad, because I tried. I refuse to compromise what I value. Not anymore."

She cradled the back of Joey's head with her hand, the feel of his downy-soft hair soothing her the way it always did.

"Joey might have been the catalyst to our current upheaval, but maybe that's also a blessing. No matter who his father turns out to be, this situation has forced us to reevaluate our lives and behavior. It's allowed us to put the focus back on what matters."

"So what you're telling me is that I managed to raise a daughter—" Garth rose from his chair and walked around the side of the desk "—who is not only beautiful, sweet and funny but also way smarter than her father."

Poppy grinned at him then stood. He wrapped his big arms around her, the way he'd been doing for as long as she could remember.

Her dad was a good man, not perfect, but *perfect for her* and, hopefully, for her mother. He drew back slightly and placed a hand on Joey's back.

"May I hold him?"

Nodding, she shifted the baby to Garth's arms. "It's going to be so difficult to say goodbye when the time comes."

"Maybe it won't come to that." Garth supported Joey's head and neck as he lifted him to eye level. "This little fella couldn't find a better mother. Although I still don't think he resembles any of us, I sense the Fortune spirit in him. He's been through more in a month of life than he should have, but he's going to be strong like you and your mother are."

He drew the baby close again and met Poppy's gaze. "You mentioned loving Joey. How do your feelings stand with Leo? Do I need to shake some sense into that boy?"

Poppy laughed softly. "You sound like Rafe. I didn't fall in love with Leo on purpose, but it happened just the same."

"Because of the time the two of you spent together caring for the baby?"

Poppy thought about the question then shook her

head. "Joey brought us together, and the proximity moved things along faster, but I fell in love with the man Leo is now all on my own. I like who he is and who I am with him. He makes me believe I'm capable of so much. I love how he sees me. I love…him."

"Like I said, Poppy-girl, you're a smart kid. But to fall for a man who can't give you what you need…" Garth trailed off.

"And you're the smartest man I know, Dad, so don't let Mom go."

She watched his chest rise and fall with the long breath. "I'll do my best, sweetheart." Poppy's phone dinged, and she took it out of her back pocket, secretly hoping Leo had reached out.

Nope. She read the text from the spa's manager, Benita, and glanced back at her dad. "Can you hold him for a minute while I put the leftovers in your fridge? Then I need to go. We're debuting a new skincare line at the spa, and the products were supposed to arrive tomorrow, but they were delivered this morning. I want to be there to organize things."

"What about Joey?" Dad bounced the baby in his arms. "Are you and Leo still caring for him together given how things stand with you?"

"Leo and I aren't anything. I'll take him with me. Everyone loves Joey at the spa, so I'll leave him in the daycare room for a bit. I'm on my own again."

"You're never on your own as long as I'm around. Joey is a cutie, and I'm here by myself right now. He can stay with me for a couple of hours."

"Did you just offer to babysit?" Poppy tried not to gape.

Garth flashed a sheepish grin. "Your mom isn't the

only person I should be treating with more care. I've
been focused on what this baby means to our family
from a DNA standpoint. But there's still the matter of
you, Poppy, and the huge thing you've done by taking
him into your home and heart."

"It wasn't hard."

"Because you are something special. I haven't recognized that as much as I should, and it's not simply about
Joey. The staff at the spa adore you. You support every
single person in this family without fail. The whole fact
that you are willing to be a foster parent says so much
about your character. I don't know what's going through
Leo's mind. But it's about him. Not you. *You* are amazing."

She bit down on the inside of her cheek to keep the
tears from leaking once again. Stupid tears. Leo had told
her she was amazing, but in the end it hadn't mattered.

"Thanks, Dad."

"Thank you for being a better daughter to me than I
probably deserve."

"That isn't how love works." She lifted up on her toes
to kiss his cheek. "You don't have to earn or do something to deserve my love. I'm happy to give it freely."

"I don't take that for granted," he said gruffly. "No
one should."

She grabbed the to-go containers and then picked
up the diaper bag from the thick wool rug to place it on
the table. "Clean diapers and a ready-made bottle are in
here. If you need anything, call or text me. I'll keep my
phone close."

Her father smiled. "Don't worry about us. I may be

out of practice, but I changed plenty of diapers with you and your brothers. We'll be fine."

"Thanks, Dad. I love you."

"Love you, too," he said.

She placed the leftovers in the stainless steel refrigerator then retraced her steps, pausing at the study's doorway. Her father stood in front of the bookcases, lined with books and framed photos of their family and past generations of Fortunes. He balanced Joey in one arm as he picked up each of the frames and introduced the baby to members of the Fortune clan.

It warmed Poppy's heart and defused the residual anger she'd felt upon waking, filling her heart with a sweetness she hadn't expected.

She missed Leo like she missed the sun on a cloudy day but knew if she waited long enough, the light would find her again. Eventually.

"Hey, Papa. How about a game of chess before dinner?"

Enzo looked up from the book he was reading in the sun-drenched living room that afternoon. "What are we having for dinner?"

Leo shrugged. "I thought we could order a pizza. The Cowboys are playing tonight, and with Mom and the girls in town for their monthly night out, it's just us."

It had been just over two weeks since the dinner that led to Enzo's setback, and Leo couldn't help but frown as he thought about how much his life had changed. And how he was right back to where he'd started.

Only nothing felt the same because he knew what he was missing. It had been his idea to get involved with

Poppy Fortune, but he never would have guessed the way she'd change everything.

"What about Joey and Poppy?" Enzo closed the book and placed it on the table next to his recliner. "Does she like pizza and football?"

Leo thought about her shouting at the refs on the TV when they made a bad call and smiled. "She likes football and sausage and mushroom pizza."

"Let's order that and get her and the baby over here."

"Sausage is too spicy for you right now, Papa."

Enzo slapped a palm on the recliner's armrest. "I'm not a toddler. I can handle some spice, Leo."

"I can't," Leo admitted with a laugh, appreciating his grandfather's instinct to retain his self-respect, even if it meant advocating for sausage pizza. "I can't call Poppy to come over."

"Why not?" Enzo asked, tone softening from his previous outburst.

Leo thought about how to explain the current state of his relationship with Poppy to his grandfather. Although making excuses or talking around the subject would be easier, he wasn't going to do that.

"Poppy and I…" He massaged a hand over the back of his neck, trying to figure out how to explain something he barely understood. "She doesn't need me anymore."

Enzo looked confused. "Why? Did they find the baby's mom and dad? Is it one of the Fortunes?"

"No. Or I should say no one knows. Her dad, uncle and cousin resubmitted DNA results but still haven't heard anything because of the backup at the lab."

"You'd think a family like the Fortunes could figure out how to expedite some results."

"I'm not sure they want to know that badly. The test results have the power to change everything."

Enzo flicked his hand in the air, brushing aside that excuse. "Then those men are cowards, and right now, they're letting Poppy do the heavy lifting. She deserves better."

"She does," Leo agreed. "She deserves better in so many areas…"

"So she *does* still need you. And even if she didn't, you want to be there with her. With Joey."

"Yes." Leo said the word slowly, testing the weight of it on his tongue. Then he shook his head. "It isn't that simple, Papa."

"Why the hell not?"

Enzo's cheeks were flushed by now, and Leo stepped forward. "Don't worry about it. I've got things under control. It's all fine."

"Don't treat me like an invalid. You look like a dog someone has just kicked in the ribs. I know you aren't fine."

"I will be."

"Don't lie to me, boy." Enzo straightened his shoulders and sat forward in the chair. "The cancer has addled my body, not my mind."

Leo moved toward the cabinet under the bookshelf that held the board games. "I don't want to worry you. Seeing you in the hospital a couple weeks ago after you'd been so upset with me at dinner…"

"Upset with you? What are you talking about?"

Leo turned and clutched the chessboard to his chest like a shield. "You were agitated when we had dinner a couple weeks ago, just the two of us. I came to check on you the next morning, and you'd been rushed to the hospital."

"You thought that was because of our conversation?" his grandfather asked.

"I know the fact that I'm still single and have no plans for that to change is disappointing. So maybe it's a topic best left alone for a while."

"You aren't single. You're with Poppy."

"No," Leo whispered.

"You broke up with her?"

"Papa, please. I don't want to talk about this."

Enzo rose and took a step toward Leo. He no longer used a cane or walker and appeared strong and stable. But that could change in an instant. Joey's sudden fever was a great example of that, and the heart attack Leo's father had suffered…

"The doctors determined that the B vitamin I was taking messed with my electrolyte balance and caused my oxygen levels to dip. It might have happened after our dinner, but that conversation wasn't the cause, Leo. You weren't at fault. I'm sorry you thought otherwise."

"You *were* upset with me."

"I have no inside voice. Your grandmother was always shouting at me to modulate my tone. I shout because that's what we do. I'm a passionate person, Leo, and I'm passionate about my family and love. Cancer doesn't change that. I won't turn myself into some mealymouthed mouse in the time I have left."

"You could never be a mouse." Despite the burning in his chest, Leo smiled at the thought. "You're the least mouselike person I know."

Enzo reached out and took the chessboard, leaving Leo feeling strangely exposed.

"And I'm wondering if *you're* a coward," his grandfather said as he arranged the pieces on the board. "It's a surprise, Leo. Not a good one."

"Ouch. That's harsh, Papa."

Enzo rolled his eyes. "You say you didn't end things with Poppy, which means she gave you the boot."

"It was more like a soft kick in the pants, but she doesn't want to see me anymore."

"Why? It was obvious how much she cared about you, and I thought you felt the same about her and the baby."

That much was true. He cared about Poppy. *Intensely.* But still not in the way she needed. Not in a way that would allow him to risk his heart.

Leo's mind whirled with explanations and rationalizations he could offer, but in the end, he stayed with his commitment to speak the truth. "She told me she loved me."

Enzo slapped a hand on the table, causing the black knight to topple over. Leo set it to rights without a word.

"That's wonderful."

"It's not. I haven't been honest with you."

"Then I think it's time to start." His grandfather sank into one of the club chairs surrounding the game table. He held up a hand before Leo could speak. "Don't even think about sugarcoating it. I can handle whatever you're going to tell me."

Sighing, Leo took his seat as well, twirling one of the chess pieces between two fingers. "Poppy was in the cafeteria when I came to visit you that morning in the hospital. She told me about Joey being left on her parents' doorstep and the fact that she'd been certified as a foster parent. I knew you'd be impressed by that."

Enzo nodded. "She's an impressive young woman."

"So much more than me," he murmured, trying not to sound petulant. Based on his grandfather's cocked brow, he failed.

"I was inspired by her. I wanted to do something that would make you happy. Make you proud."

"I'm *always* proud of you," Enzo countered.

"You also worry. You worry that I give too much to my job. You and Mom think I need to have a more well-rounded life. I need to not make the winery my only priority."

"Is it wrong that I want—"

"Not wrong. But I'm not sure it's possible. I tried because I wanted to make you happy."

"You took on the responsibility of an abandoned baby because of me?" Enzo leaned back against the leather, clearly dumbstruck.

"I know all of you worry about me, concerned I'm unhappy the same way Dad was. I love the vineyard. It's a responsibility I take seriously. I don't want to let you down the way he did."

"Your father had no head for business and even less heart for it," Enzo said. "Yes, I was disappointed, but not in him. I was disappointed *for* him because he was never satisfied when he had so much to be grateful for."

"I'm grateful and I appreciate it," Leo insisted. "Anyway, the whole arrangement between Poppy and me wasn't real."

"Maybe it didn't start that way, but I don't believe you were faking your feelings for her."

MICHELLE MAJOR 203

"Why does everyone insist on discussing feelings?" he grumbled.

"Now you *do* sound like your father." Enzo chuckled. "But you aren't him, Leo. You are your own man. We put a lot of pressure on you, maybe before you were ready. Maybe in a way you didn't want then and don't want now. It's to be expected." He exhaled slowly and waited a beat before continuing. "This vineyard has always been helmed by the oldest in the next generation. It could be time to think more about what the children of that generation want."

"I *want* to run the vineyard. But I can't help thinking if I had been more involved before Dad died and he hadn't felt so much pressure, that maybe his heart wouldn't have given out."

"You're a strong, smart man, Leo, but you are not God. I'm sorry if I made you feel like I wasn't proud of you for who you are. I didn't want you to play small in other areas of life because you were so busy taking care of his family. If Poppy Fortune isn't the woman you want—"

"I didn't say that," Leo interrupted, his fingers knotting together. "But at the moment, she doesn't want anything to do with me."

"She's not a damsel in distress. What does she want from you that you can't give her?"

"Aside from my heart?"

Enzo lifted a brow. "Someone else got dibs on it?"

"Of course not. No one makes me feel the way I do about Poppy, not even close."

"I'm a simple man, and I've got to admit I'm having trouble understanding. Do you love her?"

"Yes."

"Have you told her?"

"No, I can't tell her."

"Because…"

"Because I don't think I have it in me to love her, not like she needs."

"What are you so scared of? The girl has her own career. Her family has a business as steeped in legacy and success as ours. I don't think she's going to hold you back."

"Of course she wouldn't hold me back. She does the opposite. She challenges me to be a better person, but…"

"But what?" Enzo prodded. "Is it the baby…the fact that he's not yours biologically? Because I got the feeling that if they can't solve the mystery surrounding him, Poppy would be more than happy to become his official mommy. That's a lot for a man to take on."

"I love Joey. I would love to be his father but…"

"You keep saying *but*. I need more of an explanation."

"I'm afraid of hurting her."

"It seems to me that Poppy should be allowed to decide for herself what she's willing to risk."

"That's the problem. She's a lot braver than me." Leo gripped the white queen tightly in one hand. "I'm afraid of not measuring up. What if she realizes I'm not the man she thinks I am?"

"Become him."

Leo felt his mouth go dry. His grandfather didn't understand how hard this was on him. How much he secretly feared he could never measure up to Enzo's example. And if he tried and failed, everyone would know he wasn't enough. The idea of disappointing the people he loved—or cared about in Poppy's case—had his gut churning. "Even if I could, I don't have time for love right now."

"Make time, Leo, because nothing's more important." Enzo's smile looked wistful. "It's the one thing I can guarantee is finite."

Leo frowned. "I don't want to think about that."

"No one wants to think about it, but you have to. I'm not necessarily talking about myself, so don't start grieving me just yet. My time on this earthly plane is limited, but so is yours. No one can predict the future. I didn't expect to lose your grandmother when I did. There were times after her death I thought I would have rather followed her into the unknown than live without her."

Enzo drew in a steady breath. "But I kept living and gradually learned to love life again. We don't get to decide how much time we have. We only get to decide what we do with it while we're here. This is the only life you have, Leo. I don't know if you'll get over Poppy or she'll find someone else…"

Leo growled low in his throat. He hated the thought of her with *anyone* else.

"But if you love her, the joy of every day you have with her will be worth the potential pain of risking your heart."

"There's a chance she won't even take me back. But I do love her—" he admitted quietly.

"Then what are you going to do about it?"

His grandfather asked the question so matter-of-factly it made Leo smile despite the nerves pulsing through him.

"I'm going to convince her we belong together." He

felt lightheaded and dizzy but somehow free as he said the words out loud. "No matter what. Poppy and I belong together."

"Do you want to spend the rest of your life with her?"

Leo swallowed then nodded. "So much it scares the hell out of me."

"Then you need to stop wasting time. Make the most of every moment you have."

Enzo stood and walked to the small writing desk in one corner, opened a drawer and returned to the table with a small black box clutched in his hand.

"I knew the moment I met your grandmother that I wanted to spend my life with her."

He opened the box to reveal a familiar emerald-cut diamond set in a white-gold band with filagree on either side of the stone. "It took a few years before her feelings caught up to mine, but the day I slipped this ring on her finger was one of the happiest of my life. I hope it brings you the same sort of joy with Poppy."

"Nana's ring?" Leo stood and embraced his grandfather. "Papa, it's too much. I can't—"

"It would make your grandmother so happy, Leo," Enzo rasped, then pulled back and placed the ring box in Leo's hand, wrapping his fingers around it.

"Yes, it's a risk to let yourself love with your whole heart, but I believe the two of you are the real deal. I'd be honored if your intended wife wore this ring."

"Thank you, Papa. It means the world to me." Leo grinned and dropped the box into his pocket. "Now I just have to convince Poppy she still loves me as much as she did before I messed things up."

Enzo shrugged. "You have the Leonetti charm. It shouldn't be that difficult."

Leo hoped his grandfather was right. He took a step toward the door, then stopped and glanced at the game table. "Would it be okay to take a rain check on our chess game?"

"Anytime, my boy." Enzo winked. "Go claim your queen."

"I plan to do exactly that," Leo promised as he hurried out of the room, determined to tell Poppy what was in his heart.

Chapter Fifteen

Leo tried not to fidget as he waited on the porch after knocking. It took a few minutes for the door to swing open, and he couldn't hide his shock as Garth Fortune stood on the other side with Joey in his arms.

"Joey," Leo whispered.

"Hello, son," Garth said coolly. "What can I do for you?"

"Is Poppy here?" He tried to look beyond Garth's shoulder, but the older man wasn't budging an inch. He made a better door than a window.

"Pretty sure you're aware she doesn't live here." Garth frowned. "Were you expecting to find her?"

Leo shook his head. "No, sir. I wanted to talk to you. I just..." He reached out to touch Joey's cheek, but Garth stepped back. "I didn't expect to see you holding my... the baby."

"I'm watching him while Poppy's at work. She was going to bring him to daycare at the spa since her regular child-rearing partner flew the coop, if you know what I mean."

So Poppy had talked to her father about the two of them. He shouldn't be surprised. She was close to her family in the same way as him. He wanted her to have that support.

"Do you have time to talk for a few minutes?" he asked. It seemed prudent to ignore Garth's not-so-subtle jabs.

As his grandfather had recommended, Leo was willing to beg to earn the right to get down on one knee and ask Poppy to forgive him and be his wife.

"Who's there, Dad?"

Garth chose that moment to turn to one side and reveal both Rafe and Shane approaching behind him. Based on the glares they sent Leo, they knew what had happened as well.

"You have a lot of nerve showing up here looking for my sister," Rafe barked.

"I was looking for your father. I'd like to talk to you about Poppy and my intentions toward her," Leo told Garth.

"Oh, hell no." Shane shook his head. "You keep my sister's name out of your mouth, Leonetti."

Garth shifted the baby to one arm and held up a hand. "I'll talk to him," he said, and although both sons looked pained by the thought, they didn't argue. Leo wondered if anyone other than Shelley dared to argue with Garth.

"Can I hold him?" Leo asked, gesturing toward Joey. "I miss him so damn much."

"I'll hold the baby for now," Garth said.

Leo realized that although the head of the Fortune family had agreed to speak to him, he wasn't going to make the conversation an easy one.

That was okay. Leo had done hard things before, and nothing compared to how difficult it had been to walk away from Poppy. He'd been a fool and was determined to make things right, whatever it took.

He could handle whatever these three Fortunes threw at him. Eyes on the prize, he reminded himself. And there was no greater prize than Poppy.

He followed her brothers and dad down the hall and into Garth's office. It fit the distinguished man, with wood accents, heavy furniture and walls lined with books and framed photographs.

He wanted to take a closer look because he could see a blonde girl at various ages smiling from many of the pictures. There would be time for that, he hoped. Time to learn everything about Poppy.

"Tell me what you're doing here and why we shouldn't kick your butt," Shane interjected.

"I know I made some mistakes." Leo grimaced as he looked between the two brothers.

"Putting it mildly," Rafe muttered.

"Can Leo speak without the two of you interjecting every three words? Otherwise, we'll be here all afternoon." Garth's serious, steadfast gaze focused on Leo.

Joey, who had an uncanny ability to pick up on the mood of a situation, shoved his fist into his mouth and quietly sucked on it while staring at Leo.

Suddenly, the rehearsed explanations and rationalizations Leo had devised on the way over seemed trite and ridiculous. The thought that Poppy would consider taking him back was absurd and so out of reach that he might as well fashion wings and try flying to the sun.

"I'm an idiot," he said, remembering what his sisters had told him not to be. "I love your daughter, Mr. Fortune, and the baby you're holding like he's my own.

Both of those things scare the hell out of me because I'm not a man who expected to fall this hard. Or at all."

"For someone who professes to love my daughter, you have a funny way of showing it."

"That was fear," Leo admitted. "I'll regret hurting her until the day I die, but if she'll give me another chance, I also promise you that I will love her forever and beyond."

"Talk is cheap, Leonetti," Rafe said, and his father nodded in agreement.

"Why should any of us believe you now? Poppy has been hurt too often, but it's never been like this. She sees something in you—"

"It's the hair," Shane said, tousling his own dark locks. "He's got good hair. He may be a tool, but he's got good hair."

Leo wasn't sure how to take that, but Garth smiled slightly, so that was a step in the right direction, even if it was at Leo's expense.

"I hope it's more than my hair. I love her, and I have a ring in my pocket that I plan to ask her to wear. But first, she has to forgive me, and I want your permission before I talk to her. I've made mistakes, and I know Poppy is surrounded by a family that adores her. She loves all of you very much. I don't want to go forward on the wrong foot."

Garth lifted Joey onto his shoulder and then gave a small nod. "Okay."

Leo waited for more, but the older man offered nothing else. He glanced over his shoulder again at Poppy's brothers. Their attention was also focused on their father as if something more would be coming.

"So you believe me when I tell you I love her?"

Garth gently drummed his fingers on Joey's back as he considered the question.

"The question is whether my daughter will believe you," he replied. "I appreciate the nerve it took to come here and speak to me, given what a mess you've made of things. But Poppy is the one you'll have to convince, and I hope you do. If my daughter chooses you despite the mistakes you've made…"

He looked over Leo's head once again to his two sons. "You have the blessing of everyone in this family."

"Yeah, but if you hurt her again, all bets are off," Shane added brusquely.

Garth smiled but his dark eyes were hard. "That's true. Hurt her again, and you're finished."

Leo probably should have been offended at the veiled threat, but he felt just that protective over every one of his sisters, so he understood the sentiment.

He was glad Poppy was surrounded by people who had her back. That said, he had no intention of getting into a predicament where he would have to face any of these Fortunes again. If she gave him another chance, and he prayed she did, he wouldn't take her for granted for one moment.

"Are you going to wait until she gets home from work?" Rafe asked, stepping forward and patting Leo on the back. "Because if you think we're protective of her, her staff makes us look like one of those litters of foster kittens she raises."

Leo did not relish taking up another gauntlet or publicly acknowledging how much of a fool he'd been. But he also didn't want to wait, and Poppy deserved a public apology. He wanted everyone to know how much

he valued her. If telling her at the spa would convince
people, that's what he'd do.

"I'm going to the spa," he said, and her father nodded
again, this time in obvious approval. "Good for you, son.
I think you'll be a nice addition to this family."

"Yeah, we'll put you in charge of the wine at holiday
dinners," Rafe said.

"Gladly," Leo agreed. "But there's one more favor I
have to ask. Because as much as my feelings for Poppy
are about her, I plan for a life that includes more than
just the two of us. I want to give her the world because
she's mine. The whole of it."

"Then let's talk about how you prove that to her,"
Garth said, and suddenly Leo felt hopeful that he might
have a chance to win Poppy back and claim the happily-
ever-after he wanted more than anything.

Poppy walked out of her small office at the end of the
spa's long hallway and paused. She heard loud voices
coming from the reception area and quickly moved in
that direction, unsure about the source of the commo-
tion and wanting to deal with it before the bridal party
scheduled to come in for an afternoon of prewedding
pampering arrived.

Clients needed to be greeted with a calm, peaceful
vibe as soon as they walked through the door. She liked
to think of the spa as an oasis from stress and hoped it
would also work its magic on her.

At the moment, she felt less than blissed out, but the
morning of keeping busy made time go by faster. Her
boots clicked on the marble floor as she walked, and
she plastered on a smile that froze in place as she saw

Leo standing with Joey in his arms in the center of the reception area.

Benita, the spa's manager, and several aestheticians stood before him, looking for all intents and purposes like a white-smocked firing squad.

"What happened?" she demanded as she pushed through the line of staff. "Why do you have Joey? Is my dad okay?"

Leo visibly swallowed, then nodded. "Everything is fine. I'm sorry, I didn't mean to frighten you. I stopped by your dad's house and asked him if I could have Joey for a while."

Poppy's heart lurched at his words. As devastated as she felt that Leo had walked out, the fact that he still cared enough about Joey to want to be a part of the baby's life tempered her anger ever so slightly.

"You can't," she said, despite her feelings.

"Damn straight," someone behind her muttered under their breath. "This fella's messing with your head, girl."

Leo flinched at the words, which were not exactly said in a hushed tone.

"Do you want to go back to my office and talk?" she offered. "It might be easier."

Joey fit so perfectly into the crook of Leo's arm, and the boy cooed happily. Poppy understood how comforting it was to be held in Leo's strong embrace.

But seeing them together was making this so much worse for her.

Because whether fact or fiction, she *wanted* to believe the process of getting over him would be easier if she avoided going into town or any place she might run into him.

So as much as it hurt, she had to make him understand they couldn't see each other. He needed to let go of Joey so Poppy's heart could release him.

He started to nod, then held up a hand. "No. I'm going to do this here."

"Do what?"

"Your dad and brothers agreed that it might be my only chance of convincing you."

"What are you trying to convince me to do?" Poppy's mind whirled in confusion. "And why are you talking to my dad and brothers?"

"I'm making a mess of this." Leo ran a hand over his jaw, his gaze slightly panicked until he looked down into Joey's sweet face and his features relaxed.

"Help me out here, kid." The baby's mouth worked, but then his eyes drifted shut. Leo smiled ruefully at the boy then raised his gaze to Poppy. "I guess I'm on my own."

Behind Poppy, someone snorted. "I thought this guy was supposed to be smooth and charming. He looks like my son when he got caught sneaking out."

Leo nodded and pointed to the spa manager. "Exactly. I'm in trouble and completely out of my element."

"I don't understand *any* of this," Poppy murmured.

"Yeah, I know I'm mucking this all up, but..." He took a deep breath then blurted, "I'm scared to death I've lost you forever." He shifted closer and lowered his voice, looking so sincere that Poppy's heart fluttered in response. "I'm terrified I won't find the right words to persuade you to give me another chance."

"You want another chance?" Poppy pressed her palm to her chest, where her heart had started beating an erratic thump. "Another chance at what?"

"To convince you that I understand you are the best thing that's ever happened to me, Poppy Fortune. The morning I saw you in that hospital cafeteria will go down as one of the best days of my life because it brought you back to me. Please forgive me for being the biggest idiot on the planet...

"And the truth is, I never should have let you go the first time." He placed a hand on Joey's stomach. "This baby gave me a second chance to get things right. I owe him my heart for that. My life. Because *you* are my heart and my life."

"That's a darn good apology," Benita said.

"Next level," someone else murmured.

Poppy spun on a heel to face her staff. "Don't you all have someplace to be or work to do?"

Only to be met with a row of shaking heads.

She turned back around when the bells over the door chimed, and four boisterous young women filed into the spa. Their voices trailed off as they took in the scene before them.

"Welcome," Poppy told them. "You must be our afternoon bridal party?"

The woman in front sported a bedazzled Future Mrs. Travis T-shirt. She lifted a pair of oversize sunglasses to the top of her head. "Are we early?"

Leo didn't move, and Benita took a step forward before Poppy could answer. "No, ladies, you are right on time. Come on in. We'll get you checked in momentarily, but right now, we're witnessing something magical. Have a seat on the couch over there, and you can join in the fun."

Poppy rolled her eyes, her cheeks heating with embarrassment. "Leo and I can continue this discussion in my office."

"Not a chance," Benita told her with a bright smile.

"We're always up for fun," one of the bridesmaids offered. "Especially if it's juicy!"

Benita nodded and gave them a thumbs-up. "The best kind. Let me bring you up to speed. Poppy and Leo are fostering this sweet little baby…"

The bride nodded. "The abandoned Fortune baby. I heard about that."

Poppy suppressed a groan as Benita continued, "Yes, well, things got a little rocky between Leo and our Poppy. He made some bad choices."

"We've all made bad choices at one point or another," a petite redhead told Leo, looking sympathetic. "It's how you deal with them that counts."

"Now, Leo, tell Poppy what we're all waiting to hear."

The bridal party quickly moved to the leather couch on one end of the reception area and sat close together, clearly ready for the show.

Leo's intense gaze hadn't left Poppy. "I love you and I want to spend the rest of our lives proving how much. Please don't make me wait, sweetheart. I have to know whether I've got a chance with you."

Poppy had trouble getting the words out, the lump caught in her throat, making it difficult to speak.

"What's changed from yesterday?" she asked softly. "If this is just about Joey… I know how much you care for him, and I appreciate that, but…"

Leo studied her, visibly struggling to articulate his thoughts. "Yes, I love him but you will forever hold my heart, Poppy. You have to believe me. You are courageous and beautiful. Brilliant and strong. You inspire me to be a better man. I'm already a better man with you in my life."

She smiled and shook her head. The problem was she didn't know how to play hard to get. She didn't know how to do anything but give him her heart. But as much as she wanted to believe him, she couldn't do that if he couldn't give her what she needed.

"I love Joey so much it hurts," he continued. "If no one comes forward to claim him and the DNA tests prove he isn't part of the Fortune family, I want to raise him with you. But the most important thing to me is being with you, Poppy. It's loving you."

"But what's changed?" she insisted, refusing to settle for anything less than how she knew she deserved to be cherished.

"I have. You've shown me how valuable it is to be vulnerable, which I never thought I could be. I thought I didn't have time for love or family. That if I opened my heart, I'd be hurt. The thought of living without you is so much worse than anything else. I'm not sure I'll ever deserve the way you love so openly and how you give your heart so freely, but I'll try every day to make you happy."

His voice cracked and he drew in a shaky breath. "Any storm that comes our way, we'll weather it together. I don't know how much time we have, but I want to spend all of it with you."

"That was a darn good speech." Poppy spoke the words around the tears that she couldn't stop from streaming down her cheeks. "I love you, Leo," she whispered. "I love how you make me feel special just for being me."

"You still love me," he repeated as tears filled his dark eyes. "Even though, as my sisters would remind us both, I've been an idiot."

"My idiot," Poppy said and took a step toward him.

At the same time, Leo pulled a box out of his jacket pocket. With Joey still in his arms, he dropped to one knee. "I will love you forever, Poppy Fortune. I don't want to wait or waste another moment without you. Will you make the dreams I didn't even know I had come true and agree to be my wife?"

There was a collective gasp from the peanut gallery.

"Girl, that's a way better proposal than the one I received," the bride on the couch called out. "You *have* to say yes."

"Yes," Poppy murmured. "Of course I say yes!"

Leo slipped the beautiful vintage diamond ring onto her finger. "This is the ring my grandmother wore, and it's a perfect fit for you. I plan to love you the way my grandfather loved her—with his whole heart."

"And I plan to love you right back, Leo."

Holding her hand in his, he stood and kissed her.

The happiness Poppy found in Leo's arms filled her heart in a way she knew would last a lifetime. As her staff crowded around her and Leo for congratulations and to admire the ring, pure joy washed over Poppy like a warm wave.

She'd taken a risk to be herself and found love in the process. Life might bring challenges along with the good times, but with Leo at her side she'd make the most of every moment.

* * * * *

Don't miss the next installment of the new continuity
The Fortunes Of Texas:
Secrets Of Fortune's Gold Ranch

A Fortune's Redemption

by USA TODAY *bestselling author Stella Bagwell*
On sale March 2025, wherever
Harlequin books and ebooks are sold.